Jack Tripper Stole My Dog

A novel by

Paul McGuire

Edited by Kristin Bihr

Cover designed by Kat Goodale

Cover photo by Flickr user "eriwst"

Author's photo by Kym Bracken

Printed in the United States of America

First Printing: May 2011

First e-Conversion: May 2011

ISBN: 978-0615486345

"Happy families are all alike; every unhappy family is unhappy in its own way."

- Leo Tolstoy, *Anna Karenina*

Chapter 1

Ivan stood at the bottom of the squeaky stairwell when he realized that he forgot something. His foggy mind caused him to forget many things. The day before, he had forgotten the keys to his cab. The day before that, he forgot to mail a payment to the hospital.

Ivan retrieved his cell phone and retraced his steps down the stairs with gloomy thoughts about the impending late-summer day. He worried if the crooked mechanics at the shop finally fixed the shoddy air conditioning in his ailing cab. Six days a week, from 6 a.m. until 6 p.m., Ivan battled the boundless insanity of New York City and manned a cab through a maze of steel, concrete, and glass.

When his shift ended, Ivan rushed to his second job as a driver for the Montague Limousine and Car Service in Brooklyn. Montague Limo was owned by one of the most notorious thugs in the Russian mafia, Pytor, a.k.a the Helsinki Hammer. Pytor's reputation as a no-nonsense bookie was known. According to the legend, a trio of obnoxious and drunken sailors welched on an ice hockey bet. The Red Army's squad dominated Finland and breezed to a 3-0 victory. After the game, the sailors ignored Pytor when he attempted to collect a debt worth 100,000 Rubles. Pytor challenged all three foul-smelling nuclear sub-working grease monkeys to a fight in the parking lot of the hockey rink. It wasn't even close and Pytor sent all of them to the hospital. He assaulted one sailor so badly, that the doctor mistakenly reported the man had his head bashed in with a hammer.

When everyone discovered the truth, that Pytor inflicted the damage with his own hands, they all flinched in fear. Ever since that incident in Finland, no one dared to fuck with the Helsinki Hammer.

Ivan's brother, Yuri, ran Montague Limo for Pytor. Ivan detested working for his brother because of a never-ending family squabble that spilled across four continents and spanned three decades, leaving behind a stream of blood, countless scars, several broken hearts, scores of decapitated pets and dozens of missing teeth.

Ivan had no choice but to work for his brother on the side because he needed cash. Fast. Times were tight and the economy seemed like it was getting worse. Ivan had not had a day off in months.

Ivan's wife, Olga, constantly hounded him to work extra shifts every night and on the weekends. She embarrassed him further by begging Yuri for more shifts for Ivan. Olga bore the financial burden of paying for all of her mother's medical bills. Ivan felt that was her sole responsibility, yet he was the one working a second job.

Olga was born in the Ukraine, otherwise known as the bread basket of the former Soviet Union. The oldest child in her agrarian family of twelve, Olga inherited a long list of domestic problems after her beloved father died in a tragic, yet suspicious automobile accident. When Olga's jaundiced mother went blind from a lingering case of rickets, Olga insisted that her mother migrate to Brooklyn and move in with them.

Ivan hated his mother-in-law, calling her the "Old Mule" behind her back. He was pissed that Pytor overcharged him for a forged passport and Green Card (total cost $12,400) that the Old Mule used to gain entry into the country. Ivan was lucky that he snuck her in before 9/11, otherwise the price for false paperwork would have been quadrupled.

Ivan loathed the endless cycle of misery, working nonstop to pay for someone else's debt. It had become his sole reason for existing. That realization was utterly depressing, but instead of killing himself, he flirted with the idea of shooting Olga's mother.

"If she was a farm animal," Ivan thought, "the Old Mule would already be dead."

Ivan unlocked his cab, slid into his seat, and rubbed his sore lower back. He glanced at the fuel gauge. FULL. He couldn't remember filling the tank the night before, but was glad he didn't have to gas up because he was already running late.

Ivan turned on the radio and listened to his favorite morning show hosted by Howard Stern. That morning, Stern interviewed an aspiring porn actress from Long Island, who wanted to have a boob job in order to break into the industry. Stern was hell-bent on seeing her shaved vagina, and he offered the model $3,000 to get naked for everyone in the studio.

Ivan drove his cab a couple of blocks and double-parked in front of his neighborhood bodega. He grabbed a cup of coffee (black with three sugars) and a buttered roll. He hesitated when he saw the "Next Jackpot $23 Million" poster, but he only had a few dollars on him, which he needed to use for change for his shift.

Ivan opened the door to his cab and a young man in a wrinkled navy blue suit whistled loudly as he jaywalked across the street. The suit got Ivan's attention.

"Take me to Maiden Lane," the suit barked.

Ivan sighed, sipped his coffee, took a huge bite of his roll, and dropped the meter on his first fare of the day. He looked at the clock. 6:13 a.m.

The suit whipped out his cell phone, knocked on the partition, and asked Ivan to turn down Howard Stern. Ivan always accommodated requests. He was not bothered if riders politely asked him to lower the volume or turn off the radio. What really bothered him were groups of young kids ordering him to change the dial until he found a suitable song. Of course, they never tipped well.

Ivan adjusted the volume on the radio, barely audible enough so he could hear Howard but the suit couldn't. During commercials, Ivan listened in on the suit's phone conversation. He once got a hot stock tip when he eavesdropped on Wall Street broker. A few years earlier, Ivan invested in a software company that sold Y2K programs. Ivan bought 3,000 shares of the penny stock and within a few months the stock blew up. Ivan turned $600 into a hefty $88,000 profit prior to the dot-com bubble and Y2K paranoia. He used his windfall to fulfill a dream of finally owning his own cab. He purchased the medallion (the expensive license to legally operate a taxi in New York City) and a cab with his stock profits.

Ivan had been waiting years for a new tip, but the latest passenger was not discussing the stock market. Instead, he bragged about his latest sexual conquest.

"No, you wouldn't believe it!" the suit said, "I only went out for one drink after work, but I met a chick on the way out, a blonde, kinda like Gwyneth Paltrow with nice tits. She was plastered and totally into me, so I stayed for another drink and then suggested that she give me a hummer in the bathroom. I was joking but figured, what the fuck right? Get this… she was some sort of public sex fetishist and was totally into shit like that. But the bathroom lines were really long at that lounge, and fuck, I wanted to get my dick sucked, so we bailed. I hailed a cab and the next thing I knew, she was giving me a hand job in the back of the cab. We somehow ended up at her place, somewhere in the middle of ... shit I don't have a clue..."

The suit knocked on the partition again.

"You speaka the English, right?" the suit said without giving Ivan a chance to answer. "Can you tell me where exactly you picked me up?"

"America," Ivan said.

"OK, tough guy, I'll play along. So where in America... wait... where in New York City did you pick me up?"

"Brooklyn."

The suit resumed his call, "The Russian cab driver said I was in Brooklyn. Yeah, he's some sort of fucking comedian. I got Yakov Smirnoff driving me to work."

Ivan sipped his coffee and drove over the Brooklyn Bridge. He overheard fragments of the suit's conversation, how "they banged three times, including once in the morning," and how she was "a screamer," and how "the bitch liked getting her hair pulled" when she went down on him.

The suit tipped him $2. Ivan finished his breakfast and turned up Howard Stern, who had revealed his ultimate fantasy – to anally penetrate Britney Spears.

Ivan ignored a black man with a NY Mets baseball hat who stood on the corner of Chambers Street and frantically tried to wave him down. It's not what you thought, because Ivan did not hate black people. He liked people of all cultures, religions and colors – which is one of the reasons why he loved living in New York City. Ivan justified racial profiling because of two facts: 1) All seven men who robbed him over his 16-year career were of African-American descent, and 2) Non-whites, on average, tipped much lesser than their Caucasian counterparts.

For years, Ivan wrestled with his blatant racial profiling of customers. His only friend was Jimmy, the surly Irish bartender at the Montague Street Saloon, where Ivan was known to drink a few times a week. Ivan confided in Jimmy about his conundrum, but Jimmy reassured him that he wasn't doing anything wrong.

"Business is business," extolled Jimmy in his Killarney accent. "The business world is color-blind. There's only one color here in America... green."

"Green," Ivan blurted out when he passed the stranded black guy.

Ivan turned onto Church Street and spotted a young woman in her early twenties, flagging him.

"Penn Station," she said.

The young woman wore a black cocktail dress, the same color of her wavy dark hair. She hoped that Ivan did not notice that she had a case of really bad "bed head" and that she poorly attempted to make it right using the reflection of a parked car. She dialed her phone and tried to speak quietly, but Ivan heard everything.

"Can you pick me up at the train station?" she said, then paused for a few moments. "No, mom. Everything is fine. I missed the train last night and I crashed at Cassie's. Did you get my message?"

She hung up, wiped a tear, and then made another call.

"Hey Cass, it's me and I need you to cover for me. FYI, I told Mom that I crashed at your place last night. Just in case she follows up, because you know how Mom gets." She paused for a few seconds then continued, "No... I'm not alright. It went awful last night. A disaster. I mean I know he wanted me to do this ever since we started going out. And, you know, I really really really love him. And it's been a fantasy of mine too, but it all went so fast. His cousin was totally hot, but it wasn't like I expected. You know, doing it with two guys. I mean, it felt awkward and uncomfortable and I don't know…the whole thing felt… wrong. They seemed to be enjoying themselves, but I feel so dirty now. I wasn't really having any fun, maybe because I was too stoned or something, but I got too self-conscious when they pulled out the video camera. I feel sp used."

She burst into tears and Ivan watched in his rearview mirror as the cab sped north on Sixth Avenue. Ivan usually did not meddle in the lives of his passengers, but the young woman in distress reminded him of Sasha. He thought about asking the crying passenger if she needed help, or if she was OK. Ivan glanced at her again in his rearview mirror. She wiped her nose with a tissue and composed herself. He lost the nerve to say something. Instead, he resumed the rest of the trip to Penn Station in silence.

Chapter 2

Olga called, but Ivan never liked talking on his cell phone so he did not answer and sent his wife to voicemail. Ivan picked up an elderly German couple near Central Park on the Upper West Side. Like most cabbies, he hated airport runs, especially to Newark Airport loaded with low-tipping Europeans. After he dropped off the Germans at the terminal, he was forced to wait in a slow-moving taxi line in order to load up new arrivals. Most cabbies welcomed the breather to chat with their friends, but Ivan detested small talk with other hacks. Ivan hated all of his taxi-driving brethren; he really couldn't stand his fellow Russians and he particularly distrusted Arabs after 9/11.

Luckily for Ivan, he had stopped off at a curry restaurant in Murray Hill an hour before his airport run. The curry joint was owned by a former cabbie and gave cabbies discounts on meals and allowed any driver to use his restroom facilities. Ivan took a piss break and then bought a Lotto ticket and small carton of orange juice at the bodega next door. He also purchased a fifth of Stolichnaya at Cole's Liquor on 27th Street. Vodka was his favorite afternoon relaxer because it made time go faster. Ivan mixed all of the vodka with orange juice in his thermos, mildly amused that his favorite drink in America was named after a tool.

"If Pytor is the Helsinki Hammer," Ivan thought as he took a sip of his strong concoction, "then I am the Russian Screwdriver."

Ivan, only halfway through his first shift, shook off any exhaustion with a couple of pep pills he acquired from Alexi, the drug-peddling dispatcher at Yuri's limo service. One of the other limo drivers was a burned-out hippie who often made fun of Ivan for being the "Red who loved Reds."

In the 1970s, dope fiends referred to speed pills as Reds, but Ivan missed the joke completely because the pills were pink. The pep pills were the only thing that kept Ivan awake and allowed him to work in excess of 120 hours a week.

Ivan sipped his thermos and watched the clock. When the speed kicked in, he finally returned Olga's call.

"That daughter of yours," Olga screamed. "I do not know what to do with her! She is stubborn like her father."

"And a crazy bitch like her mother," Ivan thought, but instead he answered with his usual sounds of silence. He desperately wanted to put his wife in her place, but he let her rant for ten minutes before he hung up.

Ivan's daughter, Sasha, had moved out of their apartment two years earlier on the day after she turned 18. Sasha vowed never to return and firmly held her ground on that threat. Sasha and Olga didn't speak for over a year until Ivan convinced his daughter to call her mother on Mother's Day. The call lasted less than two minutes and was dominated by an odd silence on both ends of the phone. Ivan's idea to get his wife and daughter on better speaking terms cost him $500 – that's how much his caustic daughter demanded for the Mother's Day phone call. Sasha needed the cash to bail her delinquent boyfriend out of jail. The pseudo-punk rocker drank too much Mickey's Big Mouth and got arrested for urinating in the middle of an uptown No. 1 subway car.

The vile glue sniffer was called Slash or Slayer or Slab or something like that. Ivan had only met him twice, and he couldn't stop starring at the multiple piercings on his gaunt face.

He never bothered to get his name right because he knew that Sasha really wasn't in love. Sasha only shacked up with Slab because she needed a place to stay, so that's why she put up with his juvenile bullshit. She was using him to get what she wanted, just like Olga did with Ivan. The expression fit: like mother, like daughter.

Earlier that morning after Ivan left for work, an intoxicated Sasha called Olga and verbally abused her on the phone in a scathing diatribe in which she called her mother a cheating slut and a whore. Olga hurled the insults right back in English, Russian and Ukrainian. At the end of the call, Sasha revealed to her mother that she broke up with Slab and met somebody new – an Australian woman – and that they were engaged.

Sasha ended her fling with Slab after she caught him in the middle of a rumpus with a petite Malaysian girl he had picked her up at the dogrun in Tompkins Square Park. But that wasn't the worst of it. The girl's pug tore apart one of Sasha's sketchbooks. Slab's drummer, Yohan, the one-eyed stick-handling wonder from Reykjavik, Iceland, never stopped the pug; instead he was fiercely masturbating on their couch while sniffing a pair of Sasha's soiled panties.

A furious Sasha snatched up the Malaysian girl's pug and tossed it out the window of their five-story walk-up apartment in Alphabet City. The defenseless pooch almost hit a delivery man from Sushi World. The guy dodged the falling pug, who snapped its neck upon impact. The delivery guy marveled at the Jackson Pollock-esque splatter of the pug's blood on the sidewalk.

Sasha wasn't done. She grabbed the box of condoms that she had just bought the night before and poked holes through each of the condoms until she ruined the entire box. After she sabotaged the condoms, she sauntered past Yohan who still clutched his member, his good eye covered by Sasha's dirty underwear.

When Sasha left the building, a small, yet curious crowd huddled around the canine's carcass. She laughed uncontrollably, satisfied that her revenge ploy was complete. She bolted down the street and almost knocked over a woman exiting a boutique. That's when she met Amanda, a perpetual traveler on holiday from Sydney, Australia. From that moment, 19 year-old Sasha poured all her energy into her relationship with Amanda.

Amanda, almost twice Sasha's age, was immediately smitten by Sasha's benevolent green eyes. It was difficult for a man, or a woman for that matter, to resist Sasha's green gems. Sasha genuinely fell for Amanda's reddish hair and her angelic movie star face. She discovered a true friend, a capable lover, and a supportive mother figure she had been craving her whole life. Amanda's affluent family had amassed a small fortune selling pizza-flavored potato chips in Australia, New Zealand, and all over Southeast Asia. Amanda was financially set and helped pay Sasha's tuition for acting classes at the New School. Amanda also bought Sasha art supplies and took her to different cultural events.

Ivan had known about his daughter's lesbian tendencies since the Clinton administration. Sasha kissed her first girl when she was ten and had her first full-blown lesbian experience by the seventh grade. She was never without a boyfriend during high school, but she had many lovers of both sexes including her best friend Kelly. The two best friends rotated the location of their Saturday night sleepovers. Every other Saturday night, Ivan was lured down the hallway by the erotic sounds echoing from his daughter's room. He pressed his ear right up against the door so he could hear every moan and groan, lick and suck. He loved his daughter, and never looked at her in an inappropriate manner.

However, the thought of a pair of 15 year-old girls diddling themselves with fingers and fists got him off.

It didn't take long before Ivan fell hard for his daughter's best friend. It started on Sunday mornings when Kelly and Sasha bounced into the kitchen smiling ear-to-ear with a freshly-fucked glow. Olga made the girls omelets with Velveeta and Spam. Ivan stared at Kelly as she ate. She often stared back.

Kelly. Her name gave Ivan goose bumps. Kelly. There was not one orgasm that Ivan had in the last five years that didn't have Kelly's name written all over it, her face buried into Ivan's neck, her legs wrapped around his waist, her nails digging into his scarred back.

Kelly. Kelly. Kelly.

Ivan stopped thinking about Kelly when he reached the front of the taxi line at Newark Airport. He looked at the clock. 1:43 p.m. Two middle-aged women were directed to Ivan's cab. He took one last swig from his thermos, jumped out of the cab, and quickly tossed the ladies' bags in the trunk.

"The Sheraton, please," said the woman in a red St. Louis Cardinals t-shirt. She attempted to read Ivan's identification and picture tag that was displayed on the partition.

"Ivan Den-d-diiii…," she struggled, "Oh I can't say that."

Her friend tried with no luck.

"Where are you from?" asked the Midwestern tourist.

"Brooklyn," Ivan said.

The passengers laughed, but he wasn't joking. He had a good Stoli buzz slurping around his head and was not really in a mood to chat. Luckily, the two women chatted with each other nonstop during the entire ride into the city.

Chapter 3

Ivan unloaded the tourists at the Sheraton and collected a rare $10 tip. He picked up a new fare right away – a businessman in his late fifties, who asked Ivan to take him to an address near Columbia University. Ivan drove north on Broadway until he stopped at a traffic light on 85th Street. The man made a call on his cell phone and spoke in a language Ivan did not understand – maybe Norwegian or Swedish?

The light changed and Ivan gunned the accelerator. When his cab cleared the intersection, a black SUV with New Jersey plates sideswiped him. The driver, distracted by his phone, did not see Ivan.

"Fuck!" muttered Ivan as soon as he heard the undesirable scraping sounds of two vehicles grinding against each other. He peeked in the rearview mirror and inquired about his passenger's condition.

"You OK?"

The Norwegian nodded yes, but politely said that he was running late and handed Ivan a $10 bill. The meter read $6.25. The Norwegian told Ivan to keep the change and immediately hailed another cab.

Ivan inspected the right side of his cab and was relieved when he saw minimal damage. He wouldn't miss the rest of his shift unless he had to wait around for an hour or two to file an accident report with the police. Ivan didn't want to deal with the NYPD. He also didn't want his ruthless insurance company involved with another accident claim. He thought both were out to get him, so he avoided dealing with either entity at all costs.

A teenager scurried out of the SUV with his hat backwards, a diamond stud in one ear, and a scruff of pathetic chin hair. The kid froze when he saw the huge yellow mark running across the entire left side of Daddy's gas-guzzling SUV.

"Fucking stupid spoiled rich American kids," Ivan thought.

The kid called his father and they had a brief conversation. The kid hung up and looked at Ivan.

"Ummmm, do you speak English?"

"Yes," an irritated Ivan barked. "Do you?"

"Ummmm, my Dad said that maybe I should offer you some money to pay for the damages so that way we don't have to call the cops because maybe you are an illegal alien or something like that. Ummm, yeah, my Dad said you probably didn't want the cops involved, and that if I just paid you some cash, you know, so the insurance rates don't go up."

Ivan was pleased that the kid did not want to involve the police, but he wasn't about to let the punk off so easily.

"Ummm, so how much damage did I do? What will it cost?"

Ivan put on his best poker face and shook his head as he pretended to inspect both vehicles. His cab only had a minor scrape, nothing that a touch-up job couldn't cure. The huge dents in the back quarter panel of the cab occurred during an accident with another cab on the Fourth of July near the Lincoln Tunnel. But the kid didn't know that, so Ivan decided to shake him down.

"I should call the police," bluffed Ivan.

"No, you can't!" the kid pleaded, almost throwing a tantrum. "Don't call the cops. I will pay you in cash."

The kid fumbled through his pockets before he asked his passengers (an Eminem clone riding shotgun and a trio of jailbait girls in the back seat) to fork over any cash in their possession.

"We have almost $150."

"Not enough," Ivan barked.

"Wait! I also have an ATM card. I could go get more cash."

Ivan pointed at a Citibank branch on the corner and the kid sprinted away. Ivan hoped that a patrol car didn't pass by while he waited. The kid returned with $400 in cash. Ivan counted it all and stuffed the wad of bills into his left shoe.

Ivan successfully extorted another dumbass suburban kid from Jersey. He didn't care because it was their wealthy parents' money. Besides, what parent allowed a kid who can barely shave to drive a luxury SUV around Manhattan while blasting hip-hop and talking on the phone? The spoiled brat deserved it.

Ivan jumped back in his cab, took a swig from his thermos, and drove toward Central Park. An elderly lady flagged him down near Columbus Avenue.

"The Met," she demanded.

She unleashed a rapid-fire conversation the second she got in. Preoccupied with other thoughts, like how much it was going to cost to pound out the dents, Ivan paid no attention to the rambling lady.

"My smart and handsome nephew, Edgar, just graduated from NYU Law School and his new girlfriend works as an intern at the Met, so she's giving me a sneak preview of the new Paul Klee exhibit."

Ivan did not respond and cruised through Central Park as the old lady discussed the genius of Klee. Ivan made a right turn on Fifth Avenue and unloaded the old lady in front the Metropolitan Museum of Art. She handed him four crisp one dollar bills and two quarters for a $4 fare.

A group of three high school girls ran down the front steps of the Met and rushed over to Ivan's cab.

"Can you take us to the Village?"

Ivan nodded and the girls hopped in the back. Two of them giggled when they heard the automated voice that played every time a new passenger slid into the back seat. A recording of actress Eartha Kitt reminded all passengers to "buckle up" before she purred like a cat. Kitt played the role of Catwoman in the campy *Batman* television series. Two actresses played the role of Catwoman and were distinguishable by their race: Julie Newmar was white, and Kitt was black. When Ivan first arrived in America, he watched reruns of *Batman* in an attempt to improve his English. He became fascinated with Kitt's portrayal of Catwoman and longed to "taste her chocolate love."

The girls talked loudly so Ivan didn't have to eavesdrop.

"I can't believe that douche did that to you!" the girl in the middle screeched, "I mean how long have you two been going out?"

"Six weeks," the sullen girl said. "And he's not a douche."

"Well, if you sleep with that slut Marcy Whitney, then I'm sorry, but you're a douche. If you want to get back at him, maybe you should go fuck all of his friends. And then you should write an anonymous post on LiveJournal saying that he has the smallest cock at Dalton."

They all giggled and Ivan bit his tongue to contain his laughter. He dropped the prep school girls off at St. Mark's

Place, where they took off in search of dime bags of weed. Ivan's phone rang. He hated talking on the phone but he was expecting a particularly important call.

"Five minutes," he whispered.

Ivan parked on Second Avenue and walked to the corner of 7th Street. He opened the door to Kiev and sat down at a wobbly table in the back of the greasy Ukrainian diner. He ordered a coffee and two pierogies from the surly waitress. She made a wisecrack in Ukrainian about his foul body odor. Even though he knew exactly what she said, he ignored her and rushed down the narrow corridor to the bathroom, where he proceeded to clog the toilet. He returned to his table at the same time an athletic-looking bald man walked into the diner. He made a bee-line for Ivan and sat down across from him without saying hello. The man slid a small package underneath the table and Ivan shoved it into his pocket.

Chapter 4

"It's not a conspiracy theory," explained Tal. "It's a disinformation campaign on the internet, fueled by rumors that Israel masterminded 9/11 to draw the Americans into a Holy War against radical Islam. That's all bullshit, just disinfo from anti-Zionists. If anything, we're the ones who told you it was coming. Just like 60 years earlier with Pearl Harbor, the Americans knew about an imminent attack, but the government let it happen so they could exploit the issue politically and financially."

Ivan knew Tal through an old comrade in the Red Army. Tal, a former major in the Israeli Special Forces, also worked as a security consultant for El Al Airlines. Rumors suggested that Tal also reported to the Mossad, but Ivan didn't know for sure.

Ivan met Tal for a meal once a week but always at different restaurants in Manhattan. Ivan enjoyed Tal's fascinating stories about outlandish travels in the Middle East and North Africa. Tal combined his personal heroic travel adventures with international political affairs, and then weaved it into a monologue that would make any conspiracy theorist drool: firsthand accounts of corrupt regimes, puppets propped up by American and European oil companies, promiscuous flight attendants who acted as double agents, and a sophisticated ring of Hasidic rabbis who smuggled thousands of Ecstasy pills from Tel Aviv to JFK airport every single day.

Ivan knew very little of the state of worldly affairs. He was an uneducated man who rarely read newspapers and instead watched a lot of TV. He preferred the Cartoon Network and TV Land over the talking heads on CNN and Fox News. But he loved listening to Tal's fascinating theories about 9/11 and the massive cover-up that ensued.

Ivan's weekly meeting with Tal also had a business angle. Ivan's other part-time job, outside the realm of Yuri and his fleet of stretch limos, was doing whatever it took to earn extra money – playing poker, selling black market items, or distributing drugs. Tal had unusual connections, which allowed Ivan to acquire contraband at discount prices. During the previous four weeks, Tal gave Ivan a kilo of Afghani, unloaded a batch of stolen credit cards, and made Ivan drive out to a warehouse in Red Hook, where they boosted a dozen DirectTV de-scramblers. But that day, Tal handed Ivan two pill bottles filled with Viagra and Ecstasy.

Ivan needed the Viagra for personal use. The cumulative effect of fatigue, cheap speed, and Stoli had negatively affected Ivan's ability to perform. Sometimes, he couldn't get his little comrade to stand at full attention, like any honorable uncircumcised Russian soldier. Ivan was too embarrassed to tell Tal that he needed scientific help for an erection, so he lied and fabricated an elaborate story in which he supposedly sold Viagra to NYU students, who crushed up the blue pills and snorted them before a weekend orgy. Tal didn't blink an eye when Ivan told him that outlandish tale; he didn't care and only wanted to move his surplus.

The Ecstasy, on the other hand, was not for Ivan's personal use because he sold the pills to doormen, bellboys, and bouncers. When Ivan drove the limo, he often encountered wealthy clients with a flock of high-end call girls, all of whom were looking to party.

With the pills safely in his pocket, Ivan walked down Second Avenue singing his favorite Bee Gees song from the *Saturday Night Fever* soundtrack. He stashed the pills underneath his seat in a hollowed-out section below the rug where he kept a hunting knife and duct tape.

Ivan turned on the radio and looked at the clock. 5:06 p.m. The heart of rush hour. While most cabs vacated Manhattan and returned to garages in Long Island City, Queens to complete their shift change, Ivan drove for another hour or two. It was one of the few perks about owning his cab because Ivan dictated his own hours.

Ivan chugged the rest of his thermos and prepped for a final hour of work. He pulled out of his parking space and instantly got flagged by a young woman with bright blue spiked hair, black leather miniskirt, fishnet stockings, and a black dog collar around her neck.

"Chelsea Piers, please," she piped up in thick British accent.

Ivan nodded. The island of Manhattan was not very wide, but driving the width during Friday rush hour could take almost an hour. Ivan fought the insane congestion and arrived at Chelsea Piers almost twenty-five minutes later.

"Why blue?" he asked.

The British girl paused for a moment and answered, "I got bored with it being green."

Ivan shrugged. The blue-haired Brit stiffed him with a twenty-five cent tip. A pissed-off Ivan didn't want to wait at the taxi stand at the Piers, so he drove south down Joe DiMaggio Highway, formerly known as the West Side Highway. He made a left turn on 14th Street into the Meatpacking District, where he immediately spotted a fare. A leggy, high-heeled, full-figured woman with strawberry blonde hair and an elegant dress gracefully slid into the back seat. Through the rearview mirror, Ivan glanced at his passenger longer than usual.

"Lucky Cheng's. Do you know where that is?"

Ivan nodded yes. He knew its location in the East Village because his daughter used to live nearby.

"Life is too short," said the woman without any provocation, "You have to live and take chances, don't be afraid, don't fall victim to the comfort of conformity. Be yourself, express yourself and find out who you really are, because each day is precious and lasts milliseconds in the bigger cosmic scheme of things. But today, honey, you have to go get your own, and do it your way, right now, no more wasting time and waiting for other people to either show you the way. You need to stand up against the majority, and take action, and be who you are!"

Ivan nodded, completely unprepared for the quick and honest philosophical rant. He glanced at his rearview mirror and came to the realization that the dude looked like a lady.

The cab arrived at First Avenue and 1st Street, near the entrance to Lucky Cheng's. The drag queen gave him a generous tip and handed him a business card that read: *Leticia the Dominatrix*.

"I like the silent type," said Leticia. "You better call me."

Ivan did not respond and drove away.

"She was good looking for a man," he thought as he glanced at the clock. 6:09 p.m. He turned on the "Off Duty" light but someone ignored the sign and stopped him at a traffic light.

"Can you take us to Williamsburg?"

Anywhere else and Ivan would have ignored the request, but that destination was on his way home so he unlocked the doors. A young couple hopped in and they couldn't keep their hands off each on the ride to Brooklyn.

Usually on Fridays in late summer, traffic exiting the city was light because most of the rich people who normally took cabs at rush hour were already at their beach houses in the Hamptons. Alas, not that Friday. Ivan got stuck in a slow crawl of vehicles that finally picked up when he crossed over the East River via the Williamsburg Bridge.

Ivan unloaded the touchy-feely couple on Metropolitan Avenue at 6:42 p.m. With his shift finally complete, he smiled and turned on the "Off Duty" light. He drove a few blocks to North Seventh Street and sang along to a CD.

"Well, you can tell by the way he walks, he's a woman's man."

An excited Ivan had not seen his mistress all week. He thought of her seven times every minute because he desperately needed to see her. The timing was perfect because her boyfriend left town for a week with his band – a nefarious group of acid-chomping dread-locked freaks, who played a fusion of post-modern electronica, 1970s soul, New Orleans funk, and British Ska. The band members were a hodge-podge of Eurotrash wannabes and a sorry bunch of drugged-up hooligans, who preferred the road over steady employment and scratched their asses at the cyber critic from *The Village Voice*, who labeled them a "nomadic cult of psychedelic addicts and trust fund-hippies who successfully brainwashed art school dropouts and new-age beatniks with repetitive chromatic scales played by out-of-tune instruments and a vast array of kitchen appliances, but their burnt-out throngs of fans were too stoned to tell the difference between butchering a Velvet Underground cover and generating self-indulgent noise-pollution with a vacuum cleaner."

The band finally migrated from the hipster capital of the world, Williamsburg, to somewhere in the Green Mountains of Vermont, where they were scheduled to play an eco-friendly music festival with all proceeds donated to a non-profit foundation that saved Costa Rican primates from the destruction of the rainforest.

Ivan had planned on seeing his mistress later that evening, but he couldn't wait. It was too good to be true that his last fare of the day miraculously requested a drop off only a few minutes from his lover's loft. He parked his car a block away and retrieved a couple of Viagra pills from his secret hiding spot. He also sprayed two mini-bursts of Binaca into his mouth. He was finally ready to see his young, sexy mistress after waiting all day. The anticipation began the moment he woke up at 5:30 a.m. when he jerked off twice in the shower thinking about his angel... Kelly.

Chapter 5

Kelly had been Ivan's lover for almost four years. Neither his volcanic-tempered daughter, nor his irrational wife had a clue. He almost got busted the moment the affair ignited, a day that was always on his mind.

Ivan threw a huge birthday party for Sasha when she turned sixteen. Sweet Sixteen. Ivan and Olga rented out the VFW Lodge near Prospect Park for the only party they ever hosted. Sasha invited all of her childhood friends including her Catholic high school classmates. Ivan didn't want to invite his brother, but Olga insisted that Yuri was on the list. Even Pytor showed up. He made his nephew videotape the entire party for free, and later handed out copies of Sahsa's Sweet Sixteen to everyone in the family. It was a nice gesture that made everyone happy, but Ivan feared that Pytor might use that against him in the future and force him to return the favor in true Godfather fashion.

Sasha and Kelly had been friends for almost a decade. Kelly was born in Brooklyn to Belarusian immigrants who spoke very little English. Her father worked as an electrician's assistant in the World Trade Center and her mother worked with Olga at one of Pytor's dry cleaners (ironically a perfect business to launder his drug and prostitution money) on Atlantic Avenue in Cobble Hill.

Sasha and Kelly attended the same grammar school, but they went different high schools. Sasha, on her mother's insistence, went to St. Cecelia's Ukrainian Catholic School in Manhattan. Kelly stayed close to home and went to Brooklyn Tech. She excelled in school, but deep down wanted to be an actress even though she was gangly, awkward, and flat-chested until the "Titty Fairy" came to visit her when she turned fifteen. Despite her thin frame, in Ivan's mind, Kelly developed perfect-sized breasts. From ugly duckling to a buxom Lolita, Ivan cherished every minute that Kelly spent in their apartment hanging out with Sasha.

Olga hit the bottle hard which made her even less attractive to Ivan. He had not been in love with her since Sasha was born. But Kelly became the revitalization of love inside Ivan. It began harmlessly with light teasing and gushing compliments when Ivan would give her rides home in his cab. Ivan noticed Kelly gave him erotic stares during meals and he did everything possible to hide his erections.

The flirting escalated with a hug here and there, a peck of the cheek, and an occasional five or ten-second neck massage. The two had ascended a couple of levels of courtship and Ivan wrestled with the morality issues attached to feeding an insatiable sexual hunger for a 15 year-old girl. He knew it was wrong, but then again, she was the love of his life.

"What kind of world is this is we are denied the opportunity to be without a soulmate?" thought Ivan.

Unfortunately, destiny and fate didn't take into account statutory rape laws. Americans viewed sexuality differently, especially when it came to confused young girls on the cusp of carnal discovery. That's why the politicians created laws in the first place – to prevent sex fiends like Ivan from staining the downy innocence of sexually-charged adolescents.

Ivan was saddened that no one understood that the majority of his life's anguish would be alleviated by Kelly. Olga's selfishness and her proclivities for Bailey's Irish Cream (she drank two bottles a day) were the root of most of his misery, but even she would be devastated by Ivan's bombshell of Nabokovian proportions. And how would Sasha react to her father's lewd fantasies about her best friend? The thought of breaking his daughter's heart made Ivan weep.

A week before Sasha's Sweet Sixteen, Ivan and Olga bought their daughter a new stereo. They didn't want her to find out so Kelly's parents agreed to hide it. Ivan bought the stereo at J & R Music World near City Hall, then drove it to Kelly's apartment. It was a Saturday morning and both of Kelly's parents were at work. Kelly answered the door in only a tight Simpsons t-shirt barely covering up her pink panties.

Ivan's erection grew stiffer with every step down the hallway as he watched Kelly's ass cheeks wiggle back and forth. Ivan followed her into her parents' bedroom and dropped Sasha's Sweet Sixteen gift near the foot of the bed. Sasha sat down on the edge of the bed and his eyes were fixated on her hard nipples. Ivan froze in his tracks. She stood up and left the room motioning that he should follow. He snapped out of his trance and walked into her bedroom. With her back to Ivan, Kelly slowly pulled up her shirt. Her long, sandy blonde hair fell to her shoulder blades and Ivan noticed two freckles on the small of her back. Her smooth skin cried out to him. She slid off her pink panties and Ivan slammed the door.

They kissed. Sloppy and wet and messy all over. Her eyes were tightly shut. All Ivan could think about was that she smelled like flowers. He felt her gentle hands clutch his balding head. His hands wandered up and down her back, caressing her buttocks. She stopped kissing and he eased up on their embrace. Ivan noticed that her breasts were slightly uneven with the left one bigger than the right one. Kelly grabbed Ivan's right hand and pulled it to her left breast. Ivan twisted her nipple and she screamed. She grabbed his other hand and guided his fingers to her vagina. She moaned and Ivan looked down at one the hairiest pussies he had ever seen. Her juices dripped onto his hands and he was paralyzed for a few moments with pleasurable waves. He still fingered her while she unzipped his pants. She got down on her knees, licked the shaft of his penis, and Ivan prematurely ejaculated. He blasted most of his semen over her head. It splattered on her dresser and the wall behind it. That's when they finally heard the knock on the front door.

"Shit! Shit! Shit!" screamed Kelly. "I didn't hear the downstairs buzzer!"

Another tenant in the building must have buzzed up their unexpected guest, and they were now knocking on Kelly's apartment door. Ivan freaked out. He saw a picture of Kelly and Sasha taken at the Aquarium during their seventh grade field trip. A hot stinger seared the back of his neck and he clenched his fists. He had trouble breathing, like someone had sat on his chest. Kelly hurried to throw on some clothes. Before she rushed out to answer the door she pointed at her closet. Ivan got the hint, pulled up his pants, and hid inside.

Kelly opened the front door and found Sasha in the hallway.

"I'm bored," groaned Sasha. "Let's go to Marina's house and watch MTV. Maybe her cousin will bring over some weed and we can go to hang out in the park later."

Kelly ran into her room and dressed while Sasha stayed in the kitchen. She lightly knocked on the closet door and told Ivan to wait five minutes before he came out. Kelly and Sasha left the apartment. When Ivan heard the front door slam, he counted to 500 then exited Kelly's closet.

Ivan methodically looked around her bedroom, like any curious stalker would do if they suddenly found themselves alone in the bedroom of the person they desired the most. He went through some of her things. He snatched a pair of her panties from a laundry pile and sniffed them a few times before he retreated to the bathroom and masturbated. After he cleaned up his mess, he sniffed the panties one last time, before he shoved them in his pocket and left the apartment. Unknown to Ivan, the panties were borrowed and belonged to Sasha. She had left them behind the last time she slept over.

Chapter 6

Kelly lived with seven roommates, including her boyfriend, in a poorly-lit loft converted from an old shoe factory. She looked underneath the coffee table and found Pookie, one of her new Siamese kittens, licking an empty carton from Samui Happy Thai Palace. She tossed the kitten onto a ripped turquoise bean bag, which doubled as a bed for Simon, the Tool from Liverpool. The British-born manager of Kelly's boyfriend's band claimed the bean bag as his own crash space after his wife kicked him out of their apartment in Hoboken. Simon's wife had caught him in the stairwell of their building getting a blowjob from Pedro, a transvestite hot dog vendor.

Pedro was a Greenwich Village fixture and the subject of no less than thirty NYU Film School documentaries. He often gloated about inspiring the popular BBC television program *Franks and Beans*. He always wore fire engine red hot pants and a tiger patterned scarf wrapped around his thin neck when he sold undercooked, dirty-water hot dogs at his usual spot on Sixth Avenue and Waverly Place in the West Village. Simon stopped by one afternoon and Pedro seduced him with an extra helping of onions and sauerkraut.

Pedro cruised for NYU students and had a penchant for sexually unenlightened exchange students from Asia. Closeted frat boys were also among his favorite targets. He lured them back to his cramped Chelsea studio and spiked their malt liquor with roofies. He handcuffed the unconscious frat boys to his bed post and photographed their genitals. When they awoke, he poured hot wax from a lavender Victoria's Secret bath candle onto their testicles. He videotaped their encounters as an insurance policy. No frat boy would dare tell the police or admit to any of his friends that he got picked up by a queer hot dog vendor, who then drugged and tortured him with second degree burns on his scrotum. If they dropped a dime on Pedro, he would release the tapes.

Kelly hated Simon because he allowed Pedro to throw a party in the loft without her permission. Simon, Pedro, and a dozen trannies stayed up all night and trashed the loft. They drank wine, sniffed poppers, smoked all of the band's dope, and watched different videotapes of frat boys handcuffed to Pedro's bed.

Kelly's roommates had no tolerance for Pedro's flamboyant lifestyle, and Simon had worn out his welcome. They called a band meeting and came to a unanimous decision. They fired Simon and hired a new manager. Simon parted ways without much of a fight; however, they were unable to get him to leave the loft.

The band asked Kelly if she knew anyone in the Russian mob. They wanted to get rid of Simon altogether and plotted to scare him, just to send a firm message that he needed to get the fuck out of the loft. Even though the band outnumbered Simon 7 to 1, they were a bunch of passive-aggressive trust fund pussies afraid of confrontation. That's when Ivan came into the picture. Kelly suggested they hire Ivan, because he had military experience as a veteran of the Afghanistan War, Russia's version of Vietnam. Kelly knew that Ivan would do anything she asked because he was always eager to please her.

Two days later, Kelly found Pedro on the sidewalk in front of her building. He was curled up in a ball, hysterical and barely able to speak as he stuttered to reveal the shocking news – Simon's mutilated corpse had been found floating in the Central

Park Reservoir with a slashed throat, seven missing fingers, and a severed foot. In the most bizarre detail of the murder, Simon's head was completely shaved.

The band members celebrated, but the murder had an adverse affect on Kelly. She locked herself in the bathroom and vomited for three hours. Somewhere in the middle of the guilt-riddled dry heaves, she realized that she had become an accessory in a sinister conspiracy to commit murder.

Her boyfriend insisted that she didn't do anything wrong: "The senseless death of a parasitic bi-sexual Limey was a part of natural selection, you know, Darwin's theory about the thinning of the herd. If anything, you should be thrilled that you facilitated the removal of an undesired blemish on the fragile face of humanity."

A remorseful Kelly numbed the pain with coping aids. She didn't sleep for two days because she feared Simon's ghost would haunt her in her sleep. The band left Brooklyn and Kelly finally had the loft all to herself. She sat naked on her couch and cut up a stash of Colombian cocaine into three unequal lines on her coffee table. She inhaled two of them like an anteater sucking up fire ants for breakfast, then rubbed her nose and screamed at the top of her lungs. Her kittens freaked out and scurried to the far end of the loft. She snorted the last line, which chilled her searing body, and for the ensuing eight minutes her worries magically disappeared. She wiped her runny nose and took a swig from a bottle of Peach Schnapps.

Ivan rang the downstairs buzzer and she let him in. Ivan entered the loft and didn't waste any time with Kelly. He threw her down on the turquoise bean bag and in less than fifteen minutes, he ejaculated three times – twice inside Kelly and the third by his very own hand, which he executed in the bathroom.

An unsatisfied Kelly snorted another line. She walked down the hallway and stood in front of the bathroom door, where she listened to Ivan's groans. When he finished wanking off, he opened the door. She tightly hugged his stocky frame. Her limber arms squeezed him close to her pale body.

"Ivan, I have something to tell you," she said with her hazel eyes opening slightly larger.

Ivan farted twice then let go of her. "No. Must go to work."

"Can't you stay a little while longer? We have to talk."

Ivan pulled her into the bathroom, bent her over the toilet and prepared her for anal sex by pickling her rectum with his stubby thumb. Kelly tried to acknowledge Ivan but he quickly shoved himself into her. Kelly screamed. Ivan grunted and called her various animal names in Russian. Horse. Pig. Sheep. Giraffe. Kitten. Kelly screamed louder.

"Stop! Please stop! You're hurting me!"

She was near tears as a sharp pain rocketed throughout her body and she lost her vision. Her knees buckled and she almost fell headfirst into the toilet, only saving herself from complete humiliation by luckily grabbing a hold of the toilet seat.

"Stop! You fucking asshole!"

Ivan laughed, twisted her arms behind her back and shoved her head into the toilet. He couldn't stop. He refused to stop. He was on the verge of reaching his fourth orgasm in twenty minutes (which was not a personal record – he once recorded seven orgasms in 19 and a half minutes on Halloween in 1999, but that involved two nymphomaniac Icelandic Air flight attendants, three Viagras, Crisco, and the three golden words of porn: *Chicks With Dicks*).

As tired and distracted as Ivan was, four times in twenty minutes was something to be proud of, even if it was assisted by

Viagra. At the apex of his fourth orgasm, he flushed the toilet, which synchronized perfectly with Kelly's gurgling screams.

Chapter 7

Ivan looked at the clock. 7:29 p.m. He had thirty minutes to drive from Williamsburg to Brooklyn Heights, and he made it with seven minutes to spare. He parked his cab, opened up the trunk, and pulled his limo driver's uniform out of a black gym bag: black pants, wrinkled white shirt, black tie, black jacket, and a chauffeur's cap. He didn't like wearing the cap. He felt it made him look silly, but Yuri insisted.

Ivan stopped at a liquor store on Henry Street for a fifth of Stoli. Before he went to work, he stood on the corner and began his ritual.

"The Nectar of the Gods!" Ivan proclaimed in Russian.

Ivan drank out of a thermos in the cab because it appeared as though he was drinking coffee, but he switched to a flask when he drove for Yuri. It was more discreet and fit in his jacket pocket.

Ivan loved his silver flask because supposedly Elvis once owned it. Just how it got into the hands of a Russian cab driver from Brooklyn was an interesting story.

The flask, over 90 years old, originally belonged to a county sheriff in Mississippi during the early days of Prohibition. He got it as a Christmas present and carried it along with him at all times. The sheriff's grandmother bootlegged moonshine on her property. The sheriff employed the assistance of his cousins, all of whom were local Klansmen, to bust up make-shift bathtub gins and run off rival bootleggers in town. For over twenty years, he filled the flask with his family's special recipe – until he lost it during World War II in a crooked poker game. An unscrupulous drill sergeant cheated the sheriff out of $126. He also walked away with his pistol and the silver flask.

The drill sergeant held onto the flask for less than 24 hours. The morning after the poker game, the drill sergeant visited his mistress, the wife of the town milkman. The Milkman hated his job and left work early in protest. He walked into his house and caught his wife in bed with the drill sergeant. The disgruntled milkman shot him in the back of the head. His wife begged for forgiveness, but he shot her too. The Milkman urinated on both bodies, but not before he rifled through the drill sergeant's pockets and stole a pocket watch, his wallet, and the silver flask. The Milkman also stole the drill sergeant's car, which was technically the property of the U.S. Army.

The Milkman's wife's adulterous ways trigged one of the worst murder sprees ever recorded in the American South. The Milkman drove east and ditched his car near the state line. He killed two more people in Mississippi and acquired a new car in the process. He continued through Alabama and stopped in Mobile, where he murdered three college students and sodomized their corpses. He struck again in Montgomery, where he terrorized a group of nuns in a small barn behind their convent. The Milkman repeatedly raped the nuns before he shot all of them, one by one, face down in the ground, with hay shoved into their mouths. Their silent prayers to God went unanswered.

The Milkman fled Alabama and drove to Georgia. He went on the lam in Atlanta and shacked up at a boarding house located across the street from a movie theatre. One evening, the Milkman noticed a stunning young woman, eerily resembling his ex-wife. She exited the theatre with her date. Enraptured with jealousy, the Milkman followed them to the young woman's home. The Milkman hid in the bushes and masturbated while the young couple made out on the front porch. Ten minutes later, she said goodbye to her date and went inside. The Milkman followed the young man home, then ambushed him in the driveway.

The Milkman savagely dismembered Buck Applewhite, a.k.a. the "Golden Boy of Emory." The ruggedly handsome Buck was an academic all-American in two sports, the runner-up for the 1943 Heisman Trophy, and President of the Economics Society. Buck had just begun his first year of Emory Law School.

Buck's father, Dr. Les Applewhite, was crushed by the news that his only son had been viciously murdered. Dr. Applewhite was one of the wealthiest men in Georgia and the single largest shareholder of Coca-Cola stock. Buck's uncle, Otis Applewhite, served as Atlanta's mayor and he also played professional baseball for a decade, gaining notoriety for striking out Shoeless Joe Jackson twice in one inning. Both Dr. Applewhite and Mayor Applewhite had been grooming Buck to become the future governor of Georgia.

Buck's murder prompted the largest manhunt in Georgia's history, but by then the Milkman had fled north. The crime baffled detectives; they didn't find a murder weapon, nor could they figure out a motive, but most importantly, they did not have any suspects. An irate Mayor Applewhite criticized his nephew's murder investigation in the Atlanta Journal. The police were desperate and buckled under intense pressure to find a patsy.

The District Attorney, Boisfeuillet Applewhite, wanted to give his cousin, Dr. Applewhite, and the rest of the family closure. He devised a scheme to frame the murder on an innocent drifter named Latrell Johnson. Evidence was fabricated and false witnesses were paid off. The fix was in when the all-white jury unanimously voted Latrell Johnson, a black man, guilty of murdering Buck Applewhite. The judge, Harry Applewhite, another cousin of Dr. Applewhite, handed down a swift and severe sentence – death by hanging.

The Milkman followed the trial from his new home in Virginia. For a mass murderer, he demonstrated a significant amount of empathy when he discovered out an innocent man had died for his sins. The Milkman found redemption as an English teacher at a reform school.

A couple of years after Buck's murder, the Milkman got robbed in a Richmond whorehouse. The silver flask was among the items stolen by Bubbles, a charming, self-destructive, curly-haired harlot originally from Texas. Although she held onto the flask for thirty more years, Bubbles herself was an odd mystery. After turning tricks for fifteen years, she married a truck driver and moved to Memphis where she opened a dog grooming college. She tossed the flask in a box, which disappeared for a couple of decades in their cluttered attic. After her death in 1976, her adopted son, Reginald, found the flask while rummaging through the house in search of items to fence to feed his $30-a-day heroin addiction. He traded the flask for a small hit of Mexican black tar from his drug dealer, the Reverend Henry James.

Before he became the minister of the largest Baptist church in Memphis, Henry James served three tours in Vietnam as a Green Beret. He participated in the Phoenix Program, an assassination campaign funded and run by the CIA. Thousands of men and women all over Southeast Asia (politicians, secular leaders, intelligence officers, spies, and journalists) were classified as dangerous individuals who posed an imminent threat to the national security of the United States. They were all targeted for extermination.

Henry James befriended a few pilots from Air America, civilians on the CIA payroll who ran guns, money and dope in and out of Southeast Asia, both during and after the Vietnam War. When he returned to the States, Henry James found God and became the Reverend Henry James. He collaborated with a couple of old CIA connections to become one of the largest importers of heroin in the South. He shared the wealth and built sixteen churches for some of the poorest black communities in Tennessee, Kentucky, North Carolina, and Florida. All of his churches became the perfect front to launder drug money for the CIA.

The Reverend Henry James despised all drugs, especially marijuana, but he loved to drink. He filled the silver flask every morning with Jim Beam, which inspired him to channel the Holy Spirit. He cherished the flask so much, that the paramedics pried it from his hands after he died of a heart attack while delivering a sermon on Palm Sunday.

A paramedic stole the flask and later sold it at a pawn shop for $5. It had sat on a shelf in the shop for almost a year until it finally had an interested buyer – Ivan. He went to Graceland to pay homage to his favorite American singer, Elvis Presley. While waiting for his bus at the Greyhound station, Ivan wandered into a pawn shop across the street.

"It's 99.99% silver and it belonged to Elvis!" said the pawnbroker as he launched into his spiel. "Yes siree! This here flask is 100% authentificized property of the one and only Elvis Aron Presley. And if it ain't, I swear, heck, I'll ask myself, that the Good Lord above will strike me down now with a lightning bolt if I am lying!"

Ivan looked up at the ceiling. Nothing happened.

"$200," quoted the pawnbroker.

Ivan shook his head.

"You look like a fella who's a big fan of Elvis, am I right? So I'll tellya what I'm gonna do, I'll knock 10% off the price and I'll give it to you for $180."

Ivan handed the pawnbroker all the money in his pocket.

"Sold!"

"What a great bargain," Ivan thought, "Only $167 to own something from Elvis. This redneck is a sucker."

Unbeknownst to Ivan, Elvis never owned the flask. The previous owners included a bootlegging Sheriff from Mississippi, a card-cheating Drill Sergeant, a disgruntled milkman/serial killer, a hooker named Bubbles, Bubble's junkie adopted son, a heroin-smuggling preacher, and a paramedic with sticky fingers. And now you can add Ivan to that illustrious list of owners.

Ivan, in a full chauffer's uniform, stood on the corner in front of the liquor store. After he said his prayer to the drinking gods, he took out the silver flask and continued his ritual with a tribute to Elvis.

"One for the money."

Ivan unscrewed the top of the flask.

"Two for the show."

Ivan carefully poured the Stoli into the tilted flask.

"Three to get ready."

He screwed the cap back on.

"And go cat go."

He chugged the rest of the Stoli and tossed the empty fifth.

"So don't you, step on my blue suede shoes."

Ivan twirled around.

"You can do anything, but lay off of my blue suede shoes."

Chapter 8

Ivan carried a black gym bag that contained Viagra, Reds, Ecstasy, aspirin, heartburn medication, a flashlight, 17 pairs of latex gloves, extra batteries, a small radio, a deck of cards, a Sharpie, a Polaroid camera, a Swiss Army knife, three boxes of Trojan condoms, 15 feet of rope, a pair of socks, night vision goggles, duct tape, a coupon for Domino's Pizza, scissors, four garbage bags, rolling papers, brass knuckles, Vagisil, toothpaste, pliers, a jar of Skippy peanut butter, and a semi-automatic handgun nicknamed "The Smackdown" after his favorite pro wrestler, the Rock.

The last time Ivan used the bag was when he made Simon disappear. He didn't plan on using it that night, but carried it with him at all times – just in case of an emergency.

At the garage, Ivan walked into the office to sign in. Omar, the night dispatcher, had the pungent smell of a freshly-smoked blunt lingering on his clothes and breath. Ivan looked at his half-sunken, bloodshot eyes and asked him for the keys to the limo.

"Not tonight," explained Omar, "Yuri booked the limo for some rap star who was shooting a music video. They needed a lot of fancy cars and limos for the entire night." Omar pointed to a Lincoln town car, "Yuri has you driving a V.I.P. tonight."

Ivan didn't care either way. He wrote down the address of the client – a hotel near Times Square. Ivan climbed into the town car, popped another speed pill, washed it down with a swig of Stoli, then peeled out of the garage. He looked at the clock. 8:04 p.m. He had less than an hour. "Plenty of time," he thought.

Ivan drove over the Brooklyn Bridge back into Manhattan. It was weird for Ivan not to see the Twin Towers anchored at the end of Manhattan. He arrived at the Millennium Hotel ten minutes early, but his client was waiting for him in the lobby.

Ivan stepped out of the town car and a young man in his early twenties shot out the revolving doors. He had slicked-back brown hair, a striped oxford shirt, ripped jeans, and black cowboy boots. Ivan particularly liked his boots. The young man extended his hand for a handshake. Ivan obliged.

"Charlie O'Brien. Nice to meet you. Listen, here's the deal, just take me wherever I say, drive as fast as you can without killing either of us, and most importantly, no questions asked, got it? If you can follow those rules, then I'll hook you up with a fat tip. Whaddya say?"

Ivan nodded.

"Awesome. First stop is 74th Street and York Avenue."

Ivan looked at the clock. 8:59 p.m. He pulled away from the curb and Charlie talked very loudly on his cell phone.

"Yep, just got in, took a nap, and now I'm up…(pause)…yeah the flight was a bitch… (pause)… sure… (pause)… listen, I'm meeting Millie now, I'll call ya later."

Ivan drove as fast as he could to the Upper East Side. He almost hit two cabs and ran three red lights. Charlie didn't notice. He was on his phone and made three more calls: to his agent, to his sister, and the other to someone named Monte Carlo. When Ivan arrived at 74th Street, Charlie hung up his phone.

"Hang tight, I'll be right back," Charlie said.

Charlie walked into an apartment building. Ivan found a parking spot at the end of the block and waited 45 minutes. He spent all of that time thinking about Kelly while listening to talk radio. Charlie returned with his hair slightly messy. He was talking on his phone when he slid into the back seat. Ivan looked at the clock. 10:09 p.m.

"34th and Third," Charlie told Ivan, then he continued his conversation. "One down. Four to go. She thought we were actually going out to sushi or something. Stupid spoiled bitch. That sense of entitlement runs in her family. She was wicked pissed after I fucked her and said that I had to leave. Man oh man, Monte, I owe you one. She was a fantastic lay. Shit, I wish I could have stayed all night. But I'm on a schedule!"

Charlie hung up and leaned forward to attempt to talk to Ivan.

"Hey what's your name?"

"Ivan."

"Hello Ivan. I'm Charlie."

After an awkward silence, Ivan blurted out, "Mr. Charlie, you visit New York for work or pleasure?"

"Both. I grew up in New York, well in Westchester actually. But now I live in L.A., you know, where the Lakers play?"

Ivan nodded.

"I make movies. Hollywood movies. Have you ever seen *Charlie's Goldfish*? Well, that was my baby."

"No," said Ivan. "Good movie?"

"Well, I thought so. The critics disagreed. But they're fucking film critics. They wouldn't know art if it crawled up their ass and died."

Ivan arrived at the corner of 34th and Third, and Charlie sprinted down the street. Olga called Ivan to complain about Sasha. Again.

"If you were a better father, our daughter wouldn't be a lesbian."

"Maybe if you were not such a terrible mother, she wouldn't have left," was what Ivan really wanted to say, but he held back, as per usual.

Ivan hung up and called Kelly. She didn't answer. He walked around the car a couple of times to stretch his back. A homeless guy hit up for change, but Ivan told him to fuck off.

Charlie returned but with wet hair. He also carried a yellow pillow case with him that was filled with what sounded like bottles of beer.

"Next stop? The Cedar Tavern."

"Mr. Charlie, please tell me the address?"

"Shit, I can't remember. Ummm, it's near Union Square. Start driving and I'll find out the address."

Charlie called 411 and got the correct directions. Ivan looked at the clock. 11:41 p.m.

Ivan whizzed down the FDR Drive. He made it to the 14th Street exit in six minutes. Charlie hopped out of the town car and walked into the Cedar Tavern. Less than two minutes later, Charlie knocked on the window. A short blonde, with very large breasts that nearly spilled out of her halter top, was attached to Charlie's hip.

"Ivan, we have to go to my friend's place. Wherever that is?"

"Williamsburggggggg," slurred the blonde. "North 10th."

"Do you know where that is?" asked Charlie.

Ivan nodded. That was only a few blocks from Kelly's loft.

Charlie and the blonde went at it in the back seat. Ivan watched everything in the rearview mirror. If he was driving a limo, then his clients would be able to put up the privacy guard, but with the town car, Ivan saw and heard everything. The blonde's tongue was all over the place. It looked like she was licking the side of Charlie's face and his ears. Charlie's hands wandered. He wiggled his fingers through her curly blonde hair, and then he rounded second base with a hand up her top.

By the time Ivan reached the Williamsburg Bridge, the blonde disappeared from his line of sight. Every few seconds her head bobbed up and then disappeared. Ivan knew what was up. He had seen a thousand backseat blowjobs. The blonde continued sucking on Charlie's schlong for the rest of the ride.

The blonde scrambled to put her top on and Charlie zipped up his pants. She exited the car first and Charlie followed.

"Give me a half hour," Charlie said, before he grinned and corrected himself. "Make it 45 minutes."

Chapter 9

Ivan thought about how Sasha and Kelly's lives were more entangled than they both knew. The girls' roles had suddenly reversed. Sasha was always getting into trouble, but she had turned the corner with her recent engagement to the Aussie woman. Meanwhile, Kelly's life grew more and more complicated since her father's death. He worked as an electrician in the North Tower of the World Trade Center. He was among the many people who were murdered on 9/11, but their bodies were never recovered.

Kelly's mother went into shock for a couple of days, before she snapped out of it. Like Olga, she turned to Bailey's Irish Cream to numb the pain of her tragic loss. Nowadays, it seemed as though she completely blocked it out, like the entire 9/11 attacks never existed. Kelly handled her father's death much differently. She remained silent and stoic – an obvious front to be the emotional anchor for her distraught mother. Yet on the inside, Kelly's psyche had taken a vicious beating because she absorbed every single bad thought, feeling, and memory without letting them go. She stewed in her own boiling juices in a vast cauldron of ire and revenge. She kept a million lifetimes of hate bottled up inside. She was good about keeping things bottled up.

Kelly needed Ivan as a surrogate father and protector, but their relationship was too strange to explain to her mother, and especially to Sasha. Sometimes she felt utterly embarrassed at what she had done, which made her want to tell Sasha everything, but the further they drifted apart as friends, the easier it became to hide the truth.

Kelly and her boyfriend shared a tiny bedroom in a space that was originally designed as a walk-in closet. At least it had a door. Ivan rarely got to sleep with Kelly in her own bed for obvious reasons – none of the musicians in her boyfriend's band held actual day jobs and they were around all the time. At one time or another, they had each worked for a Williamsburg-based marijuana home delivery service called Fatty's Nugs, but they were all subsequently fired for smoking their inventory.

With the loft off limits, Kelly and Ivan arranged clandestine trysts three or four times a week. Their lovemaking sessions were relegated to quickies in the back seat of Ivan's cab. He knew a perfect spot to park underneath the Manhattan Bridge on the Brooklyn side.

Ivan and Kelly began their affair when she was still a high school student, and he drove night shifts from 5 p.m. to 5 a.m. While Olga worked at Pytor's dry cleaners during the day, Kelly often rushed home from school to fool around with Ivan for an hour before he started work. Their mid-afternoon romps always included oral sex on both ends. A few months into their relationship, Ivan introduced Kelly to the world of whips, ball gags, and role playing. Ivan had an affinity for getting spanked and Kelly curiously obliged. It didn't take very long before the two had intercourse in every room inside Ivan's apartment – in his bedroom, in Sasha's bedroom, in the kitchen, in the bathroom, in the hallway, in the hallway closet, on the couch, on the coffee table, in the laundry room, in the stairwell, on the roof, and even on the fire escape. It was astonishing that neither of them had been caught.

Sasha attended high school in the East Village and her commute from Manhattan back home to Brooklyn included at least two subways. Sasha always took her sweet old time coming home. Her habitual slowness garnered a nickname from Ivan –

the Turtle. Sasha had inherited the trait from her mother. Between Olga and Sasha, Ivan lived with the two slowest women on the planet, which meant that mornings were incredibly challenging. With Olga or Sasha locked in the bathroom for hours at a time, Ivan often relieved himself the only way he could – he pissed in a jar. One of the skills that Ivan acquired as a cab driver was the ability to urinate in an empty jar of Miracle Whip, the portable toilet that he stashed underneath the driver's seat in his cab.

And the dreaded #2? Ivan stepped out onto the fire escape and shit in a plastic bag.

Sasha rarely went home right after school because she was too busy flirting with her male classmates. Sasha knew they all loved her, and that when they jerked off at night, they almost always thought about her. She loved the attention and easily manipulated the insatiable sex drives of horny teenagers. Her suitors lavished her with gifts in exchange for hand jobs. They bought her beer, pizza, and dime bags of Mexican brick weed from the rastas in Washington Square Park.

Sasha also hung out with squatters who lived in a crack house on St. Mark's Place. They showed her how to crush up her anti-depressants and snort them like cocaine for an instant buzz. She huffed paint thinner in Tompkins Square Park, where she spent countless hours stoned out of her gourd while watching homeless people play chess for food money.

Once a week, Sasha ditched her horny classmates and the street kids for a threesome with the Tripps – an English Lit professor from NYU and his wife. They lived in an ostentatious brownstone off Washington Square Park and absolutely adored Sasha. Professor Tripp's wife loved Sasha's willingness to experiment with toys, gels, bondage, latex, and butt plugs. Mrs. Tripp was an artist and often asked Sasha to pose nude so she could sketch her. She preferred sharing young girls with her husband and took pictures of him ejaculating on their faces. She had a collection documenting the last twenty years.

Professor Tripp's intentions with Sasha were not inspired by an artistic calling, rather, he was an old-fashioned pedophile. He simply enjoyed pursuing young women.

Professor Tripp introduced Sasha to New York's swinging scene. They had become a part of a small, yet powerful group that included many prominent politicians, Wall Street bankers, and foreign dignitaries.

Professor Tripp was notorious for sleeping with his students and had bedded at least one co-ed per semester since 1990. Mrs. Tripp acquired her own reputation – she had a steady group of six or seven students and invited them over, anywhere from two to all seven at once depending upon her mood. She stripped them naked and lined them all up by penis size in her bedroom. She forced them to recite poems from Dylan Thomas, Rainer Rilke, and Emily Dickinson, while they waited for their turn to have a go at her.

Sasha's affair with the Tripps ended when she got pregnant. Professor Tripp had a vasectomy a dozen years earlier, so he knew that he wasn't the father. He was infuriated Sasha tried to scam them into paying for an abortion, so he ended their relationship.

Sasha persuaded two of her horny classmates to fund her trip to Planned Parenthood. Either of them could have been the father, but she really didn't have a clue.

* * *

With Charlie occupied for 45 minutes, Ivan walked around the corner to surprise Kelly. She was still pissed that he flushed her head in the toilet and would not answer her phone, nor the buzzer. Ivan broke the downstairs lock and banged on the loft's door until Kelly finally relented.

She let Ivan in, but refused to sleep with him until they talked. She sat at the kitchen table, but couldn't say what she really wanted to. Instead, she asked Ivan about Sasha. The two had not seen each other in weeks. Kelly knew that Sasha left Slab and moved out of the East Village, but had no idea about Sasha's engagement.

"I am surprised she didn't tell me," answered Kelly. "I know we had that stupid falling out after our boyfriends' bands got into that awful brawl at Brownie's."

Kelly smoked her third consecutive cigarette, while Ivan sipped some his flask.

"So what's his name?" she quickly asked.

"Her?"

"Her what?"

"Her name."

"Herman?"

Ivan shook his head.

"Amanda."

"Amanda, what? What the fuck are you talking about Ivan?"

Ivan paused, chugged the rest of his vodka, then told Kelly the story about how Sasha broke up with Slab, threw a pug out a window and met a woman that same day.

Kelly stood in silence, and a morose look of dejection blanketed her face. She had been in love with Sasha since they were in the sixth grade. Sasha was her first real kiss, her first real orgasm, her first real love. She was her love. Her one and only. Ivan was her lover, yes, he was but that's all he was. Kelly lived with her boyfriend but she loved Sasha in a way that no one else could ever understand. Their relationship was special and they tried their best to stay in each others' lives, but because they couldn't be very open about their secret love for each other, they were forced to keep their affection behind closed doors, limited to passionate love letters on purple stationery with little hearts dotting every 'i' in the lengthy letters.

Kelly had no problem with Sasha being with boys and men, but when it came to sharing Sasha with another woman, that's where Kelly drew the line. It was unacceptable in her mind, because they agreed not to see other women. They had been working on a five-year plan that entailed them moving to San Francisco together as a couple, then finally come out together.

Kelly cried. Ivan thought Kelly should be happy for Sasha, but he wasn't aware of their secret plan. In true Sasha fashion, she only thought about herself first, and as a result, she shattered Kelly's heart. But that's what Sasha did best – she made people cry.

Chapter 10

Charlie returned with a huge grin and a second stuffed pillowcase.

"Take me back into the city. Soho, please."

Ivan glanced at the clock. 1:19 a.m.

Charlie pulled a joint out of his pocket, put in his mouth, but hesitated before he lit it up. He leaned forward with the unlit joint dangling from his lip.

"Hey man, is it cool for me to smoke in here?"

Ivan nodded.

"I can smoke? Really?" Charlie asked again.

"Yes."

"I mean, are you sure that I can… you know… smoke up?"

An agitated Ivan's eyes were fixated on cars and cabs ahead. He didn't see Charlie holding up a joint until he turned around.

"Ah, the puff daddy," Ivan said nodding his approval. "Roll down windows."

"I love New York a lot more than L.A., but holy shit, the best weed in the world is grown in California."

Charlie lit the joint, inhaled a couple of big hits, then filled the backseat with an exhaled plume of smoke.

"This stuff I get in New York is all right, but super expensive. Man, with all this extra police and heightened security shit around the city, weed prices shot through the roof after 9/11. The stuff I just scored here is most likely a strain of Northern Lights harvested outdoors in British Columbia. It's your average Canadian import, with light green buds topped with orange hairs. Better than average stuff if you can get it for a good price in New York, but the stuff I got is a little dry. It's almost always marked up more than it should sell for, but hey, New York in the early 21st century is a marijuana sellers' market. Smack and coke are cheaper to get these days, especially in L.A., shit, I've never seen so much high-quality blow for Walmart prices in my life. But weed is so expensive on the East Coast now, that dealers are swapping kilos of blow for pounds of weed. No one used to do that! I gotta figure out how to drive a couple of pounds of Humboldt County trip weed from Northen California to NYC. The trip weed is a clone from the original strain hydroponically grown by a top-secret government-funded project. Green gold. One plant is a proverbial goldmine. A few pounds would make us a fortune and I could fund my next movie. Ah, holy shit, I'm so sorry, Ivan. I'm hogging this joint. Do you smoke? Do you want some?"

Ivan shook his head. He detested most marijuana smokers, but dabbled in hashish when he was in his twenties. The first time he ever smoked was in Kabul, Afghanistan during his a tour in the Red Army. He enjoyed the calm feeling even though it made him dizzy at first. His hands and arms felt calm and quiet, and all the bad voices in his head went to sleep. When he closed his eyes, he thought that he was dreaming, but he was not asleep, so he must have been caught in the place between sleep and dreaming, sort of like a hash-induced lucid dream. But then the hash took a downturn and he overanalyzed everything. It dragged him to a very dark place, which scared him. Ivan always had peculiar thoughts that he never shared with anyone because if he did, then he would not look ordinary. He kept those things hidden in a darkened corridor inside the hallways of his mind, the place where he repressed the worst of the worst memories.

He could see all of them carefully filed away into compartments which were then locked away inside secure boxes. Sometimes, he saw the faces of the people that were attached to those boxed-up memories of anguish. He looked into their eyes and felt their pain, and every bit of torment they experienced because of him. The pain transference freaked him out completely and he tried to evade them, yet he always found an excuse to explore unlabeled boxes filled with those nasty things he did not dare speak of during dinner conversations, nor the things he would ever reveal to his comrades in the Red Army. The hashish overpowered Ivan and it frightened him so much that he never wanted to go back to that mental prison.

Charlie told Ivan that most of his friends had enlightening and profound experiences during their initial experimentation with marijuana.

"I'm jealous," Charlie explained. "My first time smoking weed was ordinarily retarded. I got stoned in the back seat of Tommy Miller's mother's station wagon one night after a group of friends went to the movies. I didn't feel a thing, but Colleen Sullivan puked all over me. I picked popcorn kernels out of my corduroys for days afterwards."

Charlie passed Ivan the joint, who surprisingly took a decent-sized hit before passing it back to Charlie.

"Blueberries?" blurted out Ivan.

"Yeah, it kinda has that berryish aftertaste. Good call, Ivan."

Charlie toked a couple of hits before passing it back to Ivan, who took a long drag and coughed. Ivan handed the joint back to Charlie and made a gesture that he didn't want it back. Ivan grabbed his silver flask, but it was empty. He forgot that he polished it off at Kelly's.

"Wow, that's a cool flask," Charlie said.

Ivan smiled. "It belonged to Elvis."

"Get the fuck out of here!"

Ivan nodded.

"Never pegged you as an Elvis freak. You know the government killed Elvis? They also whacked John Lennon and Kurt Cobain."

"Mr. Charlie, you like Ecstasy?"

"Do I drop Ecstasy? Vitamin E? Rolls? Molly? E-Bombs? Happy Pills? Fuck yeah. Why? Do you have some?"

Ivan nodded.

"Holy shit, Ivan. Why didn't you say so like four hours ago?"

Ivan shrugged his shoulders.

"How much do you have?"

"How much you need?"

"Shit, I dunno, like five? Wait, make it eight. No... how about ten. That sounds good, right? You can never have enough E. You know what, make it dozen. A whole 15."

After Ivan crossed over the Williamsburg Bridge, he pulled the car over on Delancey Street and opened up the trunk. He sifted through his black gym bag and found the Ecstasy. He counted out 15 pills, which he concealed in two used Peppermint Patty wrappers.

"How much do I owe you?" Charlie asked.

"$400."

"What? Are you serious? For 15? Can't you give me a break?"

"Discount included," joked Ivan.

"I only have $300 on me. I'll give that to you now, and I'll hit up an ATM on my next stop."

Charlie fumbled inside one of the stolen pillowcases and popped open a warm bottle of Fat Tire. He unfurled one of the wrappers and popped two pills.

"Man, I definitely needed this, Ivan. I'm fucking beat and I gotta see two more girls before the night is over."

"Mr. Charlie, you told me not to ask…"

"Ivan let's just say, I am trying to do something I never did, but always wanted to do… have sex with five different women in one night."

Ivan almost got into an accident because he turned around and stared at Charlie in amazement. Charlie put his hand in the air then wiggled all five fingers.

"Yeah that's just the beginning. I'll tell you more after this stop."

"Five?" thought Ivan. "Wow. The most I had was maybe two in a 24-hour period. I don't think I've done five in one year, well, unless you count hookers, then yes. But that was over a full year. And Mr. Charlie was doing that in one night? May I live vicariously through you?"

Chapter 11

Ivan parked in front of a loft on a secluded block adjacent to Spring Street. His client was about to have sex with his fourth partner in less than seven hours. Charlie O'Brien impressed Ivan, who became instantly star-struck at the pot-smoking, womanizing, ecstasy-popping filmmaker. He looked at the clock. 1:57 a.m.

The joint Charlie shared with Ivan had an adverse effect because Ivan spiraled into a series of over-analytical flashbacks from his deviant childhood growing up in the Pasku District of Moscow. Ivan had horrible luck with the ladies. He tried, but despite his efforts, young Ivan never found the right girl. Afflicted with atrocious timing, he constantly fell in love with the wrong girls.

"You're a hideous boy," Ivan's mother reminded him many times a day. "And you eat a lot, so you have to settle down with a woman who is a good cook. Marry the first woman who shows you any attention."

Ivan never listened to his mother. He hated her. She was the local gossip queen in their sterile concrete apartment complex made up of three adjoining run-down buildings. He hated the fact that his mother knew everything and everyone. He often wondered if she really worked for the KGB, because she saw and heard stuff that the KGB never knew existed. Anotoly, the grubby man on the fourth floor, may have hidden his secret lifestyle from the Party, but he was not able to conceal it from Ivan's mother. Anotoly liked to be tied up and beaten by his wife, who regularly thrashed his buttocks with frozen scrod. His wife was no angel either – she was involved with the building's porter, a half-wit from Siberia named Yuri. Although Yuri was not the brightest guy in the Soviet Union, he was considered by many to be the dumbest person living and breathing in Moscow. Kids waited for hours in the most frigid of temperatures to tease Yuri on his way to work, as he slowly limped down the street with an unusual gait. They snickered at his left foot, often seen dragging behind him like a wounded animal. A rumor, originated by Ivan's mother, suggested that a Siberian black bear mauled Yuri's leg. One of Ivan's classmates told him that Yuri got shot in the foot by a bus driver, who had caught Yuri in bed with both the bus driver's wife and his 76 year-old mother.

It was no coincidence that Yuri, the limping Moscow Moron, bore the same name as his older brother. Ivan shivered in disgust when he thought of the possibility that the Moscow Moron fathered Yuri. Or what was worse? Witnessing a crippled idiot hump his mother, a woman resembling a 345-pound sack of potatoes? Or the high probability that the crippled idiot was his real father?

Ivan's abrasive mother beat him senseless with both a belt and a tsunami of discouraging verbal lashings. Ivan's father, an alcoholic, impotent violinist, sat idle and laughed while his wife whipped their unruly children. Ivan's three brothers sadistically tortured him, but none of that compared to the weekly abuse from the old woman who lived in the apartment above them. The old woman with false teeth made out of balsa wood paid Ivan a few pennies to do odd jobs for her. Ivan often cleaned her apartment. He dusted the shelves, waxed the floor, read the newspaper to her, and wrote letters for the 86 year-old Babushka (even though Ivan was a horrible speller). One afternoon when Ivan was around eight, she ordered him to drop his pants. At first he hesitated, but she held out two shiny new pennies and that caught his attention. With the sparkles of the new pennies in his eyes, young Ivan dropped his pants and she took a long pensive look at his genitals. She reached down and touched them, nodding in approval.

"You're dumb as a stump, ugly as an old shoe, but boy, you have a cock that is as wide as a paint can," she said and reached down to stroke his penis with a wry smile that exposed her false teeth. "You have a bigger dick than all of your brothers."

Ivan's heart raced. He began sweating and he felt something going on with his penis. He got hard like a hockey stick, but it felt weird.

"And you're even bigger than Yuri, the Moscow Moron," the old woman whispered in his ear, as she took off her underwear.

For the next decade, the old woman molested Ivan several days a week. As the years passed, Ivan wanted to break it off, but the old woman threatened to tell his mother the one secret she didn't know about. A furiously frustrated Ivan decided he had enough and pushed the old lady down a flight of stairs. She broke her neck and shattered both her legs, but survived the fall. Luckily for Ivan, she had a heart attack in the ambulance and died en route to the hospital. The old lady's last words were "paint can."

Ivan cried every day for three months but was confused because he thought that murder was supposed to make you a man. If anything, Ivan felt more embarrassment that he targeted an elderly woman for his first kill. The more Ivan cried, the more he realized he had fallen in love with the old lady.

Ivan's twisted childhood made him sad, so he tried to snap out of it by thinking about a happier time in his twenties after he returned home from the Afghanistan War. Ivan thought about his first wife, Misha, the girl with the lovely smile, lonely eyes and the red curls. Misha's father was the local police captain, a very strict man who actually liked Ivan, which was rare because nobody really liked Ivan (except the old lady who lived above him, but he knew that was only because of his large penis, and the police captain never saw his package, so Ivan was convinced the man genuinely liked him). The captain encouraged Ivan to take the police examinations because that would earn him a decent salary. The captain liked Ivan because he treated his eldest daughter with respect. Ivan never hit her or cursed in front of her. He acted like a gentleman and got her home exactly on time, as requested by her father.

It seemed like a perfect situation, except that Ivan was secretly in love with Misha's blind sister Petra. Petra's blindness was the most important thing to Ivan because she could not see what other people saw. She could not see his frayed clothes – patched-up hand-me-downs from his older brothers. She missed the pattern baldness that plagued Ivan since he was nine. She never saw his unsightly double chin or the coarse lumps on his forehead (the ones that he supposedly acquired when his mother was seven months pregnant and got beaten with a broomstick by Ivan's inebriated father, who had the justification to go berserk after he caught her fellating Yuri, the Moscow Moron).

Petra never saw the sporadic burn marks and unhealed scars on Ivan's back and arms that he incurred in Afghanistan after his Red Army unit got ambushed by the CIA-funded Mujahidin rebels, who fire-bombed his transport vehicle in Kabul. Even though he got out of the attack alive, Ivan continued to suffer from his war injuries, but Petra never witnessed the sluggish manner in which Ivan moved from room to room, like an old man who had just shit his pants.

Most of all, Petra never saw the lack of confidence in Ivan's dour eyes, or the sunken feeling of not belonging that was noticeable in his facial tics and expressions. Meanwhile, the positive attributes of Petra's blindness made her more attentive to Ivan's sincere and nurturing side. Deep down, Ivan was a warm, gregarious, humorous, simple man who listened to bootlegged American music like Johnny Cash and Elvis Presley. He loved to sing songs in funny voices, which made Petra giggle and laugh, which in turn made Ivan feel loved because they both got high on the special attention that they paid to one another.

The Captain happily arranged a marriage between Ivan and his dreary overweight daughter, Misha, but he was oblivious to the fact that Petra and Ivan had fallen in love.

Ivan, Misha, and Petra often took walks in the park on Sunday afternoons, but the hefty Misha was often out of breath, so she stopped for long rest breaks on benches. She encouraged Ivan and Petra to enjoy the park while she took a nap and rested. Ivan and Petra ditched Misha. They rushed into a secluded wooded area where they sipped vodka and fondled each others' genitals. For several months, Ivan and Petra continued their Sunday mating rituals in the bushes while an exhausted Misha napped.

Petra abruptly halted the routine when she discovered that she was pregnant. If the Captain found out that Ivan knocked up his blind daughter only a week before his nuptials to Misha, he'd drag Ivan downtown to one of the horrible Moscow city jails. Ivan would most likely be tortured and maimed, and if he were lucky, he'd get killed quickly before the Captain's thugs dumped him in Gorky Park, where the brutal winter wind would whip against his badly beaten naked corpse.

When Ivan thought he'd have to answer to the Captain, he was ambushed by a new twist in his love triangle. Petra told Ivan that she could not identify the actual father because it could have been one of any of her four lovers: 1) Ivan, 2) his brother Yuri, 3) the other Yuri, a.k.a. the Moscow Moron, or 4) her father, the Captain. None of the other lovers knew about each other. A stunned Ivan felt betrayed, but he still insisted that he would break off his engagement to Misha and marry Petra instead.

Petra couldn't figure out what to do. Unable to come to grips with her situation, she jumped off the top of one of the tallest apartment buildings in the neighborhood. Instead of a wedding, the family gathered for a funeral. Misha and Ivan postponed their wedding by a month, but even then, the event seemed subdued. A grieving Misha had lost her only sister. A confused Ivan had lost the only woman who really saw him for him. Even Ivan's brother Yuri was crushed because he also lost the girl that gave him the best fisting of his life.

Ivan and Misha relocated to Leningrad to escape the misery of Petra's suicide. He found a factory job making weapons for the military, but the change of scene did not solve his melancholy. Even the birth of his son, Nikolai, could not make him feel any better. He missed his true love Petra, and every night before he passed out drunk, he whispered her name. Petra. Petra. Petra.

Misha had grown miserable and bitter, just like her mother and her mother's mother and her mother's mother's mother had grown after a few years of marriage. Ivan was no better and hated everything. He hated the weather. He hated his job. He hated his life. He hated his wife. He hated his son, who resembled his mother more and more each day, and most of all he hated his boss, Pavel, a skinny nebbish-looking man.

Ivan hatched a plan to seduce Pavel's wife as payback for Pavel treating him like shit at the factory. Ivan got her drunk one night and she surprisingly did not rebuff his sexual advances. She requested to be hog-tied and he even urinated on her at her insistence.

Ivan taunted Pavel by leaving anonymous notes on his desk. "Your wife liked it when I fucked her in the ass and wiped it on your face towel. She loved it when I pissed on her and she licked most of it up too."

Pavel's wife got too disgusting for Ivan because of her affinity for deviant hardcore S&M, which freaked him out. He only wanted to degrade his boss by fucking his wife, but she had gone too far. Instead, he switched his focus to his boss's daughter, an unattractive high school student and easy target for Ivan because she had no experience with men. The poor girl got sucked into Ivan's web of revenge, fueled by anger, rage, and constant anti-Semitic propaganda from the Communist Party.

Disaster struck when Misha stumbled upon Ivan's affair. She found him passed out drunk on their living room floor with Pavel's homely blindfolded daughter tied to their bed. Misha attacked the young girl and beat her face in with a shoe. Misha then took a dump on Ivan's stomach, as his slumped vodka-infused body laid motionless.

The young girl's squeals eventually woke Ivan up. He had blacked out and regained consciousness with feces covering most of his body. Ivan searched his apartment and couldn't find any trace of his wife or son. Misha's clothes, his son's things, and all of his money were gone. He found a note:

Dear Ivan,

Nikolai and I are returning to Moscow to live with my family. I am going to tell my father everything about what happened, and how you tie up little girls and torture them with candlesticks. The KGB will probably send you to

Siberia for hard labor, if my father does not cut off your
balls and feed them to the rats that live in the basement.
You are a bad drunk and a terrible husband. The next
time I want to see your lumpy head, is when we bury your
ugly body. Signed, Misha

Ivan spent the next year eluding the KGB all over Eastern
Europe. He hustled and turned tricks in various Turkish bath
houses for cash and food money, before he migrated to the Ivory
Coast. He became a mercenary for the government and fought
peasant rebels on the outskirts of the capital city. Ivan eventually
got hired as a deckhand on a ship transporting cocoa beans to
South America. He jumped ship in Argentina, then paid his own
way from Argentina to Mexico (via Brazil and Panama). Ivan
practically walked over the Mexican-American border (in
actuality, he hid in the back of a truck filled with bananas and
marijuana). Although he made it onto American soil, he had
blown his entire wad sneaking into El Paso, TX. A penniless
Ivan broke into a church and stole enough money to pay for a
Greyhound bus ticket. One-way to New York City.

Ivan finally arrived in New York and ended up in Brighton
Beach. Within a week, an old friend from the Red Army set him
up with a couple of Russian mobsters (associates of Pytor the
Helinski Hammer), who secured him a new last name, a fake
Green Card, and even a drivers' license. Ivan passed the test to
become a cabbie and picked up a New York City hack license.
He'd have to drive a cab for 12 hours a day, every day, for almost
a decade before he paid off his debt. But for the first time in his
life, Ivan smiled because he was a free man. That's when he
formulated a new dream – to own his own taxi cab.

Chapter 12

Ivan fell asleep in the car waiting for Charlie. He dreamed about being the mayor of a small town in Sweden, where the townspeople presented him with bouquets of flowers and freshly-cooked hotdogs. The children sang songs in Swedish, English, and Russian. They exchanged chocolates with one another and little girls wore pink ribbons in their hair. The military generals gifted Ivan a gold-plated sword that said he had the biggest cock in all of Scandinavia.

Ivan woke up to Charlie tapping on his window. Ivan rubbed his eyes and let Charlie inside. He looked at the clock. 3:08 a.m.

Charlie got into the front seat and punched Ivan in the arm.

"Sleeping on the job, eh?"

"My second job."

Charlie apologized. "Sorry, I didn't know. What else do you do?"

"Taxi driver."

"Wow, that's sucks working so much. Don't worry, I'll hook you up with a fat tip. You've been awesome tonight, Ivan. And we have just one more stop. Upper West Side."

Ivan turned on the car's ignition and drove away.

"Wherever you got this Ecstasy from, it's really good. I mean it's awesome. I feel so warm inside and all the street lights have a fuzzy glow around them."

Charlie finally clued Ivan in on his plan.

"I'm supposed to get married on Sunday night in Connecticut."

"Congratulations."

"Not so fast. I'm supposed to, but I'm not going to marry that lying slut. My fiancée has been sleeping with one of her business managers for three months now, and this wasn't the first time she's cheated on me. She also slept with a reality show reject. I have it on videotape, too. It made me sick, but that wasn't the truly incriminating part, because she spewed venom and said awful things about her sisters, parents, and friends – and I have it all on tape. But on Saturday night, at the end of the rehearsal dinner, I'm going to show everyone a short film that I put together. They think it's a tribute to the love of my life, but instead, I'll show everyone the secret video of her sleeping with another guy and slamming all of her friends and family. I can't wait to bust her. I've been plotting this for months. Her father is going to be pissed. He's one of those Connecticut hedge fund dickheads who dropped over $500,000 on the wedding reception. I can't wait to see the look on everyone's faces when they realize that their spoiled little princess was also a fucking lying whore."

Ivan didn't believe what Charlie told him. "He must be joking, or just wasted on Ecstasy," he thought.

"That's Part 2 of my plan, which will take place tomorrow at the rehearsal dinner. You helped me with Part 1 tonight, which was me seeking revenge by sleeping with as many women as possible since I caught her. To date, I've banged 21 different women and you're about to drive me to #22. I even took a few Polaroids of a couple of USC sorority girls sucking my dick. I also banged a couple of high-class hookers during my bachelor party in Vegas. Sad to say, but I even went hogging with a fat Denny's waitress named Bertha."

"New York no have Denny's," blurted out Ivan.

He no longer had doubts about Charlie's plan. He couldn't decide if it was the craziest thing ever devised, or the worst thing he'd ever heard of – to ruin your own wedding like Charlie intended.

"So when I got to New York City, I decided to fuck five women: my fiancée's sister Millie, a hooker, a couple of ex-girlfriends, and the one girl my fiancée hates more than anyone in the world – Zoë, her roommate from college, who stole all of her boyfriends, mainly because she gave better blowjobs and swallowed. So now, I'm off to see Zoë, which I never would have been able to do without your Ecstasy!"

Ivan kept shaking his head.

"Oh!" shouted Charlie, "I never told you the cherry on the top of the sundae! The big bang? My encore performance? Once I'm done with Zoë, I'm going to wake up my fiancée right away in our hotel room citing that I'm freaking out with cold feet. I'm gonna bluff her and say I'm walking unless she blows me on the spot. She'll do it to prevent herself from the embarrassment of a cancelled wedding. Then at the rehearsal dinner, I'll reveal that the last place my dick was before she put it in her mouth, was up Zoë's ass."

Ivan laughed. Loudly.

When Ivan reached the final stop, Charlie tipped him $200. Ivan handed Charlie one of Yuri's business cards with his own number scribbled on the back.

"Ivan, you are the coolest cab driver I ever met, man. And I want to thank you for making one of the best nights of my life become a reality. Thanks for Vitamin E! Can I hug you right now, man?"

Ivan and Charlie embraced.

Chapter 13

Ivan overslept. He showered quickly and dressed, cursing all the things he wanted to do before his shift started at noon. He rushed downstairs and reached his cab without forgetting anything. He drove to Williamsburg and found a spot in front of Kelly's loft. He looked at the clock in his cab. 10:50 a.m.

Ivan popped a Viagra and called Kelly. She was groggy when she answered the phone, but insisted that Ivan could only come up if they didn't have sex. Ivan was pissed because he wasted a Viagra pill.

Kelly let Ivan into the apartment and she begged him to cuddle with her in bed. Ivan resisted initially, but finally gave up when he realized that he wasn't getting laid. Ivan shed his clothes and spooned Kelly, with his erect penis poking her in the back.

Kelly wanted to tell Ivan about so many things, but she didn't know where to begin. She stayed up all night rehearsing how she was going to tell Ivan that she was pregnant.

When Ivan finally showed up at her loft, she grew anxious and began to cry. She ate a Valium to calm down. Her tears swelled, the volume of her whimpering grew sadder, her shaking intensified and her body flailed more violently. She lost all control as Ivan sat on the edge of the bed, mired in confusion. He wanted to do something, but he didn't know how to help.

"We have to talk, Ivan."

When Kelly thought she had mustered up enough courage to tell Ivan about the baby, she instantly became a muttering and blabbering ball of emotion. She also wanted to tell Ivan that she was still heartbroken over losing Sasha, and that Sasha's engagement bothered her immensely. She also wanted Ivan to know that he really made her feel happy. He called her "kitten," which gave her goose bumps every time he said it. He made her melt. But she couldn't get out any words, which were tangled together inside her head.

Ivan squeezed Kelly tight for four plus minutes. He never let go and Kelly nearly passed out by the sheer force of love that exploded through her. She had never seen Ivan act so nurturing and affectionate before. She knew that he rarely kissed his wife in public and only occasionally hugged Sasha. But something was different. Ivan's hug was infinitely better than sex with her loser boyfriend, who could barely get it up half the time and when he did, he ejaculated in less than thirty seconds. She held onto Ivan with every ounce of frantic energy she had in her depressed body.

"Thanks for the best hug I've ever had," Kelly said, the only thing she mumbled before Ivan left.

Ivan exited the loft singing loudly. He didn't notice his excessive volume because he was tripping on Ecstasy. He accidentally took a pill out of the wrong bottle. The blue Ecstasy pill resembled a Viagra, but Ivan never bothered to check the difference before he popped the pill in his mouth.

Ivan turned on the radio and pulled out of the spot. At the first red light, he looked over at the clock. 12:03 p.m. Ivan had never been on Ecstasy before. He had no clue about the potential side effects, which included excessive hugging. The hug of all hugs he gave to Kelly should have been a warning sign. Even Kelly was a little suspicious, but Ivan hadn't a single clue what was pumping through his veins.

Ivan instinctually drove over the Williamsburg Bridge and into Manhattan to start his 12-hour shift. He began to sweat profusely when a young couple flagged him down on the Lower East Side.

"Union Square," said a tall wiry young man with a ponytail as he slid into the backseat followed by his wife, who wore a beautiful purple flowery dress. Her curly hair reminded Ivan of his first wife, Misha. He had a warm feeling in his heart when he saw the lady with the curls. He wanted to hug her.

"You are a very beautiful couple," Ivan blurted out.

The couple laughed and playfully kissed one another.

"Sometimes," the guy sarcastically replied to Ivan, "But thank you. I can't take any credit for the looks part. It's all her. She's the beautiful one. I'm just the brains."

"And the ego," interrupted the lady with the curls, as she slid her hand into her husband's pants. The husband retaliated and slid his hand underneath his wife's purple dress. The lady with the curls rarely wore underwear, so her husband had quick and easy access to her vagina. She unzipped her husband's fly and inserted her hand inside his pants.

"Are you married?" asked the guy.

Ivan nodded.

"Twice," he wanted to say, but kept the thoughts to himself. "But I was too scared to be alone, that's why I got married to women I wasn't in love with. I was afraid to be alone."

The couple slowly jerked each other off while Ivan drove north.

"Olga would be happier if I was dead," thought Ivan. "She just keeps me around for the money. Otherwise, she would have left years ago. Misha left me because I cheated on her. Ah, I

73

made a huge mistake. I was young, confused, and had a hot head."

The lady in the purple dress bit her tongue to keep from screaming after she had been brought to orgasm by her husband's four fingers that wiggled their way inside her.

Ivan dropped off the young couple at the south end of Union Square. He waved goodbye to them. He really adored the lady with the curls. He looked at the clock. 12:24 p.m.

Ivan loaded a new fare instantly. Two very good looking men, whom Ivan initially thought were gay, but were actually religious fanatics.

"Rockefeller Center, please."

Ivan looked them over. They both wore shorts, Tevas, and "Jews for Jesus" t-shirts. They carried a couple of messenger bags filled with religious pamphlets and flyers explaining the mantra of the "Jews for Jesus." One of the religious freaks offered one to Ivan.

"Do you believe in God?"

Ivan laughed. He often asked himself that question.

"I'm convinced there is no God after I almost got killed in Afghanistan."

"Even after you were not killed? Don't you think the Lord's hand had a little to do with that?" the other freak asked.

"No."

Ivan knew that the Jesus Freaks never visited the Russian military hospital where he recovered from his injuries. The screams from the burn unit kept Ivan awake at night and those shrieks continued to persist until this day. Ivan found no traces of God in the hospital. Nor could he find God in many other horrible places he frequented – whorehouses in Mexico, bath houses in Turkey, dog fights in Minsk, street brawls in Brighton Beach, and caves in Afghanistan.

"God is everywhere," explained the Jesus Freak. "It sounds to me that you are lacking faith, my friend. Perhaps you would like to join a peaceful prayer meeting we are having tonight at 8:30 in Central Park. 'Jews for Jesus' is not for Jews or for Christians. It is for people who want to find meaning within their lives through Jesus Christ. God is everywhere."

"Where was God on 9/11?" barked Ivan, to which both Jesus Freaks did not have a prepared response.

Chapter 14

Ivan unloaded the Jesus Freaks at Rockefeller Center. They blessed him instead of a giving him a good tip. Ivan got stiffed, but he was rolling too hard to notice. He looked at the clock. 12:47 p.m.

Ivan stopped for three tourists in front of St. Patrick's Cathedral. They wanted to see Ground Zero.

"Nothing to see," Ivan insisted.

"Can you take us there anyway?"

A couple of times a week, tourists requested a ride to Ground Zero. After 9/11, with the exception of the Empire State Building, Ground Zero had become the most popular tourist attraction in New York. Hardcore patriotic Americans wanted to see the impact crater that kicked off the next Holy War, while conspiracy theorists wanted to see the scene of the crime for themselves.

The family from Podunk, Minnesota in the back of Ivan's cab was no exception. They planned a vacation to New York City specifically to visit Ground Zero. They had seen all the sights: Times Square, Rockefeller Plaza, the Statue of Liberty, the Metropolitan Museum of Art, the Empire State Building, the United Nations, Central Park, The Bronx Zoo, and Tom's Restaurant and the Soup Nazi (both joints made famous from *Seinfeld*). Ground Zero was the last landmark on their list. They wanted to be among the hundreds of gawkers who posed for pictures.

"Were you working that day?" asked one of the tourists sporting an 'I Love New York' t-shirt.

"Yes," answered Ivan, who purposely did not elaborate. At the time, Ivan was on his way back from JFK airport crossing over the Brooklyn Bridge when the second plane hit. Ivan had a fare that was supposed to stay at the Marriot at the World Trade Center, but Ivan decided it would be safer to drop him off at a different Marriot in Midtown. When the subways shut down, a stream of people tried to hail his cab. Millions were stranded without any transportation out of the city. Ivan drove to Sasha's apartment in the Village. Although they barely said anything to each other, Ivan stayed there all night and watched TV with Sasha and her roommates, including the Icelandic one-armed drummer from Slab's band, who instantly declared that the Twin Towers attack sparked the beginning of World War III.

Ivan had savagely fought in Afghanistan against many of the same rebels who supposedly orchestrated the 9/11 attacks. He knew that America was doomed and eventually headed into another quagmire like Vietnam.

"Why do they want to know about 9/11?" wondered Ivan. "It was a very scary day. The worst day in the history of America."

New York City was a not-so-safe place when Ivan arrived in 1982. At the height of the crack cocaine epidemic, Ivan got lost in a couple of dodgy neighborhoods, where he was lucky to escape without his cab carjacked by crackheads.

Since its low point at the end of the 1970s, New York City gradually improved. Once Mayor Rudy Giuliani took office, the streets and public spaces were sparkling clean. Crime substantially dropped off after Rudy cracked down on "quality of life" offenses. Prior to 9/11, New York was a really nice place to live. Ivan had not been robbed in almost two years and he drove his cab at night without any problems. After 9/11, Ivan trusted no one, especially tourists who wanted to take photos at Ground Zero.

Ivan unloaded his passengers at what would have been the foot of the South Tower. The Minnesota tourists gave him a generous tip. He drove off and glanced at the clock. 1:13 p.m.

Ivan loaded a Korean girl on Broadway. She requested an address in Flushing that he wasn't familiar with, but hoped she'd give him better directions once he got into Queens. She sat in silence the entire ride and didn't mind that Ivan blasted Johnny Cash's *Greatest Hits*.

Ivan dropped off the quiet Korean girl and luckily picked up a return fare to Manhattan. A group of teenagers wanted to go to a movie theatre near Times Square. They were rude and obnoxious the entire drive, but that didn't bother Ivan one bit. The Ecstasy made him more tolerant.

At Times Square, the teenagers filed out of the cab one by one. The last teenager paid the fare with a shitty $1 tip.

"I think someone left this here."

The kid handed Ivan a copy of *Gysana*, a novel by Mona LaVigne. Ivan never read the book, but it got made into a movie starring one of his favorite actresses, Jamie Lee Curtis. He loved the movie so much he saw it twice, even though he did not understand the themes all that much. He was not a fan of postmodern feminist literature, nor a fan of hysterical women beating up men with strap-on dildos to avenge previous wrong-doings by the entire male race. He loved Jamie Lee Curtis' huge rack, though, and got to see her naked. He put the book in his glove compartment and looked at the clock. 2:28 p.m.

Ivan found all kinds of items left behind in the back seat of his cab. Cell phones and umbrellas were the two most popular lost items. Over the years, Ivan found eyeglasses, Palm Pilots, sunglasses, pens, mittens, hats, scarves, loose change, wallets, purses, teddy bears, credit cards, Metrocards, baseball hats, briefcases and backpacks. He once found a fairly new laptop computer, which he took home to Brooklyn and used to download Chicks with Dicks flicks from his favorite Danish porn site. His passengers left behind books of all kinds: art books, children's books, cookbooks, phonebooks, Stephen King books, self-help books, no less than nine Bibles, and one copy of the Koran. Passengers dumped newspapers all the time: the Daily News, the New York Times, the Wall Street Journal, the New York Post, the Village Voice, the New York Press, Newsday, the Financial Times, the Sun, and even El Diario.

Ivan often found personal mail of all kinds including a letter from a young woman to her mother stating that she was going to kill herself because her boyfriend had just left her. Ivan still carried that undelivered letter in his glove compartment and wondered if the woman committed suicide.

Ivan also discovered random left-behind items like a bag of marijuana, vials of crack, several bottles of pain killers, a knife, an unloaded gun, and a shopping bag filled with Victoria's Secret underwear, which he gave to Kelly. The most bizarre item that Ivan ever found in the backseat of his cab? An entire bucket of Kentucky Fried Chicken, including a biscuit.

Chapter 15

Ivan stopped at a light in Times Square and marveled at the lack of originality from wide-eyed tourists who snapped the same fucking photo. It didn't matter if they were from Kansas City, Milan, Johannesburg, or Tokyo, because everyone took the same picture of Times Square for relatives back home.

A bald middle-aged man, with thick black-rimmed glasses and a beige Member's Only jacket, stood in front of the ESPN restaurant. He flagged Ivan down and ran up to the window.

"Can you take me to Cyrus City on the Planet Sion? I have the proper currency and documentation."

The bald man showed Ivan a wad of fake money and gave him a Blockbuster membership card.

"No," said Ivan, who rolled up his window and sped away as the bald man cursed at him in an alien tongue that resembled Danish.

Ivan only took fares that were traveling within this solar system. He felt bad for the guy. He usually drove the crazies straight to Bellevue. Ivan always rejected anyone who requested alien planets. He hated going to Staten Island, so why would he go to Planet Zippy?

New York City cabbies have one of the riskiest jobs in the world. Any passenger could be a potential serial killer. The next person on a street corner who raised their hand to hail Ivan's cab could be sentencing him to death. In the previous 16 years, Ivan often found himself in grave, dire, serious, hairy, and fucked-up circumstances, like the time he once got shot three times by a 13 year-old assailant.

Despite the dangers associated with his job, Olga had no problem with Ivan risking his life. She always nagged him to find more lucrative work, even though that meant he was contracted out by mafia-type associates which often put him in harm's way. She was never happy when Ivan turned down side jobs for Pytor, but Ivan detested being used as muscle. He was getting too old for bag man duties, collecting delinquent payments from many of Pytor's degenerate gambling clients. Ivan hated bodyguard work, because it drew him into a nonsensical territory war between two rival factions of the Russian mafia. The young kids were wanna-be gangsters who sought out respect from the older mafioso-types, many of whom were former KGB henchmen that conducted business in a particular manner. Alas, those two groups constantly butted heads and Ivan grew tired worrying about what horrible atrocity could happen next in an endless game of retaliation. The ebbs and flows of internal power struggles within the Russian mafia were similar to the stock market – lots of ups and downs, but with more losers than winners.

Ivan's two driving jobs were killing him slowly. His back had become a twisted knot of constant pain. Alas, he had no choice. What kind of job could an uneducated Russian immigrant secure? Ivan was damn lucky to have any job, let alone two. His brother Yuri put things in perspective with a line that Ivan often repeated, "Shitty job in America beats the best job in Siberia every day of the week."

Ivan hated working the second job, but the alternative was sitting around his depressing apartment with a shitfaced Olga and her Ukrainian mother on her deathbed. Ever since the Old Mule moved in with Ivan, she dominated the remote control on the TV. He no longer got to watch some of his favorite shows: *The Brady Bunch, Seinfeld, Friends, Dark Angel,* and *The Real World.*

Although Ivan hated working nonstop, he enjoyed driving around the city because it reminded him of the Johnny Cash lyric, "I've been everywhere." In a single shift, Ivan often covered the majority of New York from Times Square, Central Park, Chinatown, Riverdale, Greenwich Village, Park Slope, Hamilton Heights, Astoria, the Lower East Side, the Upper West Side, and Soho. Whenever he drove through Chelsea, he passed bubbly drag queens and flamboyant fairies embarking on their fabulous jaunts around town in high heels, wigs, falsies, and layers of makeup.

Driving around the city was much easier than working the assembly line in an unventilated Leningrad factory, and a thousand times better than active duty as a soldier in Mother Russia's Red Army. If Kelly was Ivan's lover, than the streets of New York City had become his mistress. On his saddest days, his favorite streets cheered him up. He adored the lush greens of the tree-lined streets of Fifth Avenue along Museum Mile and often long-hauled tourists who didn't mind the extra sightseeing. He often got an erection when he sped down the FDR Drive. He loved driving through Central Park when it was open to traffic, and he tried not to hit any enthusiastic joggers or sweating bikers as they whizzed by nannies of all nationalities and colors, who pushed strollers with bright, shiny, glistening white babies.

Ivan really didn't mind the traffic all that much because it gave him a chance to think about life, daydream, or watch pretty ladies from all over the world. He loved to stare at them and imagined if they shaved their vaginas.

Ivan drove around in an invisible bubble, the perfect vantage point to observe everyone walking around him, shuffling off to work, shopping for presents, and going about their daily lives. He loved being a cab driver in the greatest city in the world instead of a being chained to a desk in a flimsy cubicle. Some days, he drove through the skyscrapers and looked up in bewilderment because each window was a gateway into someone's world, where suits fondled secretaries and some actually had lunchtime quickies in their Midtown offices. He wondered about the Big Swinging Dicks on Wall Street who crank-called their co-workers in London. Those arrogant assholes never saw a good deal they didn't have any problem with lying, stealing, cheating, bribing, raping, and mutilating to get it done.

The cab allowed Ivan to interact with people from all walks of life: doctors, tailors, prostitutes, hackers, Vietnam vets, gynecologists, insurance salesmen, date rapists, copy boys, salesclerks, chemotherapy patients, art students, dental assistants, paralegals, sleeper cell terrorists, dog walkers, soup kitchen workers, deadbeat dads, sugar daddies, struggling actors, flower arrangers, alcoholics, museum security guards, illegal aliens, ice cube chewers, lounge singers, gold diggers, potheads, lobbyists, grave robbers, elevator operators, massage therapists, nail salon workers, ophthalmologists, retired iron workers, bail jumpers, Hooters waitresses, window washers, politicians, tourists, librarians, compulsive masturbators, plumbers, receptionists, bagel butterers, piano players, docents, cartoonists, tax cheaters, pilots, neurotic suburban housewives, cheating housewives, lonely housewives, scorned first wives, pill-popping housewives, shopping-addicted housewives, trophy wives, mail order brides, knocked-up brides, and drugged-out hippies on their own magic carpet rides.

Ivan crossed paths with fellow foreigners from Belgium, New Zealand, Egypt, Cambodia, Nigeria, Peru, Norway, Italy, Sri Lanka, Greece, and Macedonia. He drove around Americans from tony suburbs like South Orange and Scarsdale, and picked up wide-eyed yokels from small towns like Cedar Rapids, Kenosha, and Lubbock. He routinely encountered people who grew up on islands: Hawaii, East Timor, Haiti, Cuba, Jamaica, Ireland, and Trinidad & Tobago.

Ivan didn't allow religion to get in the way of providing them a service. He drove people who practiced every possible religion on the planet: Islam, Southern Baptists, Jews for Jesus, Hare Krishna, Orthodox Jews, Druids, Jainists, Capitalists, Zen Buddhists, Shintos, Moonies, Anglicans, Rastafarians, Hindus, Presbyterians, Lutherans, Reform Jews, Christian Scientists, Deadheads, Phisheads, Sikhists, Conservative Jews, Taoists, Catholics, Voodoo, Scientologists, and hundreds of other smaller cults and tribal religions.

Ivan also dealt with people struggling with all forms of mental illness including the semi-normal, sexually deviant, troubled, clinically insane, moderately crazy, suicidal, seasonally depressed, mentally lost, totally gone, jaded, vanished, not from this world, Canadian, and just fucking nuts.

Sometimes Ivan closed his eyes and tried to imagine what everyone in the city was doing at that exact time. He pictured Canal Street in Chinatown at the height of mid-afternoon as tourists mixed with immigrants who peddled their cheap goods. He saw a horde of single moms and Spanglish-speaking children, who darted in and out of 99 Cent stores in Spanish Harlem. He overheard an aging yuppie couple discussing Sartre's influence on Tony Blair's stance on Iraq, as they casually shopped for California wines and Nova Scotia lox at Zabar's on the Upper West Side. He pictured all the rich pretty people enjoying their privileged lives – including surgically-enhanced waifs named Sutton and humorless stiffs named Tad, properly attired in catalogue clothes, as they mindlessly chatted on their cell phones, ignoring their other supper guests from snotty prep schools in Connecticut, the breezy ones who "jetted in from Provence" just to catch up with old chums, who themselves helplessly morphed into despicable characters from the *Great Gatsby* that Holden Caulfield scorned and plotted against. They didn't blink at a $1,800 bill for a three-hour long six-course meal as they decadently sipped $100 glasses of Champagne. They became the one thing they said would never become – vapid Randian capitalists – who ignored the plight of dozens of homeless people panhandling in front of the hipster fusion restaurant of the week – a Guatemalan-Canadian-Icelandic-Nigerian-Cajun tapas bar on the Upper East Side.

On the other side of the island on the avenues and streets that crisscrossed the East Village and Lower East Side, the bourgeoisie finally woke up late in the afternoon. Those glassy-eyed junkies, the militant lesbian squatters, crusty hustlers, and cynical pimps finally hit the streets and bummed smokes and loose change from pedestrians. The younger wave of cyber beatniks and jaded artisans cancerously peppered the oversaturated East Village with their vile minds and ill-tempered souls. They were paralyzed by an existentialist war of attrition between the power brokers and champions of idealism. Those ego-driven, self-fulfillment-preaching aimless sheeple were blinded by the eternal struggle between progressive consumerism and dwindling individualism. As a result, the freshly tattooed and pierced poseurs sipped lattes and nibbled on mango scones at the packed Starbucks on St. Mark's Place. Irony always presented itself when self-proclaimed rebels to conformity wore a duplicitous combination of Salvation Army-bought clothing and Prada shoes, as copies of *Steal This Book* and *Manufacturing Consent* bulged from their messenger bags. They talked endless shit about media-wide fascism and more shit about the drudgeries of suburban capitalism, yet they childishly needed Mommy and Daddy's credit cards to buy sushi and pay for yoga classes. They incessantly complained that America destroyed young artists, but they couldn't wait to watch the next episode of *Surviving American Fear, Real Millionaire Idol of the Anna Nicole Smith Show* or whatever reality show the lobotomized masses religiously followed, that the cool kids blogged about on the Internet, and that the mass-media tentacle of the Military-Industrial-Entertainment-Complex shoved down our throats. Staunch vegan anarchists, who were the same hypocrites that whined about the lack of ingenuity in our entertainment industry, sat huddled together in a circle jerk and burned sage and healing incense to ward off the negative vibes, yet they still foolishly forked over $12 to see another Reese Witherspoon cookie-cutter film. The worst that Middle America had to offer had moved to Williamsburg with the lost generation of scorned hipsters and bitter artisans that included avant-garde experimental photographers, insomniac writers, misunderstood musicians, out-of-work sculptors, narcissistic performance artists, lifeless dancers, obscure comedians, and conceited actors.

Interactions with auras from people from all over the world deeply affected Ivan. Sometimes, depending on the energy of his passengers, he felt more connected to the world than anyone else in New York.

Every single day, Ivan heard about other peoples' struggles, because angry and distraught people loved to tell complete strangers about their problems. Besides, a ride with Ivan was much cheaper than a visit to a psychiatrist. Listening to the daily misery of his passengers almost always made him feel better. Despite the language barrier and the socio-economic rift between himself and the majority of his passengers, Ivan found a way to identify with everyone, because they too also had endless money problems, volatile family issues, and unresolved childhood traumas. Their shared misery gave Ivan a greater sense of self-confidence, individual achievement, and a deeper appreciation for his luck, health and his life on Earth.

Chapter 16

Ivan looked at the clock. 4:21 p.m. All afternoon, he battled back and forth from being extremely hot and sweaty to totally calm and content with the world around him. Ecstasy still pumped though his bloodstream and his entire body tingled.

Ivan picked up two Italian women shopping in Soho. He fell in love with one of the girls' beautiful green eyes, which were like swimming pools of thousands of shades of green. Ivan ogled at her green eyes in his rearview mirror and got an erection. Hunter Green. Winter Green. Irish Green. Light Green. Dark Green. Hooker Green. Yellow-Green. Blue-Green. Opaque Green. Heather Green. Kelly Green. Booger Green. Jade Green.

Ivan's next customer wore a trench coat in the middle of a sunny August afternoon. The old man had a terrible sneezing fit and ripped five consecutive ear-piercing sneezes. His boogers, snot, and germs exploded all over the partition and the backseat. He continuously asked Ivan to turn up the air conditioning – when it already ran on full blast. He requested Lincoln Center, but demanded that Ivan not drive up Broadway. As much as this guy would have normally irritated the germ-conscious Ivan, he really wanted to give the old man in a trench coat a hug goodbye.

Ivan never got a chance to clean out the back of his cab before he loaded another fare – a nerdy-looking guy, who could have won a Bill Gates look-a-like contest. He asked Ivan to drive him to Columbia University.

"You look like the computer guy, Bill Gates."

The nerdy man sheepishly replied, "I get that a lot."

"Is it nice to look like someone famous? My wife looks like one of *The Golden Girls*."

"Which one? Betty White?"

"No."

"Rue McClanahan?"

"No."

"Estelle Getty?"

"No."

"Well, that leaves Bea Arthur."

"Yes."

"Bea Arthur, really? You wife looks like Bea Arthur?"

"Yes."

"My condolences," Bill Gates said before he laughed. "You know Bea Arthur was a spy? She worked for the CIA."

"Not true."

Bill Gates leaned forward and continued, "Yes. She was. So are most important people in Hollywood like the heads of the studios, producers, and directors. Most Hollywood film companies are fronts for the CIA. Steven Spielberg is huge up in their ranks. Talented as they come, but he works for *They*."

"They?"

"Yes. *They*. *They* who control the world. *They* who control the banks. *They* who orchestrated 9/11. I'm surprised you're not familiar with *They*."

"Never heard of them."

"Not them. *They*."

Bill Gates inspected Ivan's hack license.

"I'm presuming based on your name that you're Russian."

"Da."

"So you know all about repressive governments trying to control information. Well, America in 2002 is no better than Russia in 1982. Our newspapers and TV news programs are propaganda wings for big-business entities that control the politicians. It's the men pulling the strings on those puppets in Washington who make up the nefarious collective known as *They*.

"*They* control the world?"

"Now, you're catching on."

"Bush, the father, he doesn't control the world?"

"Not exactly, but his friends do. And they utilize Hollywood to help shape public sentiment. Why not? Think about it. What is the one medium that is still the most dominant in the world? Not the Internet and computers because more than 75% of the world cannot afford one. It's not print media and journalism because over half the world cannot read, and more than half of the world's population lives in countries where freedom of speech and the press is sequestered at all costs. Humans are mass brainwashed with subliminal messages embedded into television and movies. It's the easiest and most cost-effective way to brainwash the populous. *The Wizard of Oz. Field of Dreams. Old Yeller. Harry Potter. Spider-man. Beverly Hills Cop. Corky Romano. Charlie's Goldfish. Star Wars. I Still Know What You Did Last Summer.* All of that mind-numbing entertainment is a necessary political conspiracy to prevent the have-nots from seizing power away from the haves. Movies and television are also cleverly-disguised vehicles for product placement. Their entire goal is to transform society into mindless consumer-driven slaves who complete 99% of the work for a mere 5% of the profits, but then quickly piss away their profits on material items.

It's an endless cycle of consumer slavery that we're unable to break free of, because everyone's brains are too fried to do anything about it. Mind control shaped the world we live in. The Charles Manson Murders. Jim Jones. Waco. Oklahoma City. Ruby Ridge. Columbine. Princess Di. John Lennon. 9/11."

Ivan shook his head. "I don't believe you."

"Look here's the deal," explained Bill Gates. "I don't care if you don't believe me because we're all fucked. Humans are a cancer upon this Earth and we must be stopped otherwise all of the world's resources will be consumed within two generations. At the rate of exploding technology and medical advances, the world's population will double by 2050. By 2500, there will not be enough sustainable resources for humans to live. We reached Peak Oil in America in the 1970s. Right now, politicians in Washington in cahoots with the mainstream media, are trying to sell the public a second war in Iraq. What the hell do you think that's all about? Oil. And the war in Afghanistan? It's not about terror."

"The poppy fields," interrupted Ivan.

"Yes, you're correct to some extent. The Russians originally invaded in 1979 to seize the poppy fields. They gained control of the manufacturing and distribution of heroin in order to fund the Cold War, where Moscow desperately lagged behind the Americas in overall defense spending. A broke Russia looked to dealing heroin in order to fund their ballooning military budget."

Ivan finally understood what Bill Gates was talking about.

"But the real reason we're in Afghanistan is not because of Al-Qaeda's role in the 9/11 attacks. That's just a cover, a superficial reason spoon-fed to the American public to give our military an excuse to take over Afghanistan. It was necessary to go in there to build a massive trans-Afghanistan pipeline to transport oil from the Caspian fields all the way to the Indian Ocean, where the oil would then be shipped to China, who is a bigger oil junkie than America. China lacks the technology and resources to build their own pipeline. However, the Union Oil Company of California, doing business internationally as Unocal, could build a pipeline provided they had the cooperation of the Afghani government. When the Taliban-run government wasn't recognized by the U.N., the U.S. military went in, blew everything up, and handed over power to a new puppet – who just happens to be related to one of the consultants to Unocal."

"I think you're fucking crazy," blurted out Ivan.

"I don't care what you think about me. You should probably pay more attention to the fact that you're being deceived on a daily basis. The biggest threat is your unwillingness to open your eyes to the truth. Ever hear of Eugenics? A cabal of old rich white guys decided that their prime directive is to reduce the world's population to 500 million people. That's a reduction of over 90% of the world in order to preserve the Earth, and have enough oil and fresh water left over for everyone. Well, those men who make up *They* are concerned with population explosion. They're working fast to eradicate the upward swing of birth rates. First of all, *They* mass sterilized the majority of the Third World and also released manufactured diseases like AIDS. Be careful about a new bug coming out soon that will make the Black Plague look like a case of the sniffles. The new super plague will wipe out most of South America, Sub-Saharan Africa, and Southeast Asia. Heck, the Chinese have been working with American scientists and Swiss geneticists to create a new virus that will be able to wipe out billions of people. When they get close to running out of oil, rice, and drinking water, that's when they are gonna release it. On their own people!"

"When is the virus coming?"

"Oh, I have no idea, but when the first few people start dying, just remember you heard it from me first."

Ivan nodded.

"And the bankers in power have been pushing for more wars. Most of *They* are members of the banking elite who became rich by loaning corrupt leaders of fledgling countries billions of dollars, which the despots in turn used to buy weapons and tanks from other members of *They*. Those scumbags often financed both sides of a war. It happened at Waterloo, during the Revolutionary War, and again in America during the Civil War. The biggest banks operating right now on Wall Street loaned money to both the Brits and the Nazis to fight each other during the earliest days of World War II. The future wars will be more dangerous. We're already seeing how this so-called war on terror is taking shape. But that won't matter compared to the Holy War that our country volunteered to fight, which is just a different way to spin the Oil War. In a decade, the first Water War will break out when countries decide to fight over access to fresh drinking water. I'm actually looking forward to the inevitable war between Russia and China, after a despondent China runs out of oil. Their only alternative is to march into the 'Stan' countries that make up the Caspian states and seize all of the Russian oil fields. And then there's other major conflicts, like India and Pakistan that can flare up at any moment. Don't forget, *They* own businesses that profit solely on warfare, such as selling advanced weaponry to nations at war. The most diabolical truth is that many of the men who call the shots, also own businesses that profit solely on warfare. Those men are neither pro-Israel or pro-Islam. *They* are neither for North Korea or South Korea. None of them care about the freedoms set forth by the forefathers of America. Those men who make up *They* are dedicated to keep the population down and expand their families' wealth at all costs. That's why there will be a lot of wars, man, oh man, nuclear wars, chemical wars, biological wars, cyber wars. It's all coming. By the end of the decade. You'll see. The Middle East and North Africa will be a hot zone. The world is going to explode very soon, and we're all sitting around ignoring all the signs."

Ivan shook his head again and didn't believe what he had just heard. He wanted Bill Gates to stop, but part of him wanted to hear more.

"*They* are comprised of some sick fuckers, who fuck with people for pure enjoyment and sport. *They* drive around in unmarked vans and pick up homeless men to hunt, just like in that Jean Claude Van Damme movie. Ironically, the writer, producer and director of that film were all mysteriously silenced, a.k.a. murdered by *They* for using the mainstream media to expose their group. Those same weirdos picked up hookers for mind control experiments and used homeless subjects to test new drug therapies and conduct operations inserting implants and internalized communication devices. The next time you see a crazy homeless man on the street talking to himself, well, he's not really crazy because he's got one of those implant chips in his brain. He's actually communicating with the voices in his head. Fucked up, huh?"

An amazed Ivan thought Bill Gates finally made sense.

"Ever wondered what happened to all of those young women who were abducted in shopping malls? Or what happened to runaways who were picked up at bus stations? They were hand-picked for an underground sex slave ring. The better-looking girls were used as currency to buy yachts, ski lodges, elections, and Presidential pardons. I don't even want to get into the brutality and horrific details of the fates of millions of missing children all over the world who got caught up in the international sex-trafficking trade. It makes me sick to think about what *They* did to the Milk Carton Kids, you know, all those missing kids who were snatched by unmarked white vans driven by henchmen for a powerful ring of pedophiles. It makes me furious the media has full knowledge of these atrocious events, yet, they're too afraid to speak up. *They* can make you disappear anytime, anywhere. That's why I'm leaving America and moving to Iceland."

"Iceland," agreed Ivan.

Ivan reached Columbia University and Bill Gates handed him a $5 tip. He looked at the clock. 5:45 p.m.

Chapter 17

Ivan loaded two women near Tom's Diner. They requested Park Slope, which made Ivan happy because his bowels were rumbling. He lived on the fringe of Park Slope, so he knew he could go home and shit in his own bathroom.

Ivan glanced in the rearview mirror. Two lesbians were in the middle of a heated conversation. The louder stout-looking woman had a shaved head, a bull ring in her nose, and a poorly-designed tattoo on her left arm that displayed – Born A Dyke. Ivan found himself somewhat attracted to the other woman with dirty-blonde hair that jetted down the sides of her pointy shoulders. She wore black cargo pants with her round breasts snuggled tightly behind a wife-beater t-shirt. Ivan caught a sneak peak at one of her nipples shooting out. He loved New York City in the summer.

"Fuck Camille Paglia!" yelled the bald dyke.

"You would," giggled her girlfriend.

"With a 14-inch King Kong dildo! I also want to anally rape that evil cunt face Ann Coulter. I wanna lace up the strap on, fuck her doggie style, grab a hold of that bleach-blonde hair and yell, 'Yeah bitch, who you calling a dyke now!'"

They both giggled, even Ivan, although he had no clue who either Camille Paglia or Ann Coulter were.

"Seriously, there are no good female writers these days," the girly lesbian whined. "The only ones getting published are chick lit novelists."

"I thought Elizabeth Wurtzel had promise until she got too full of herself and sold out to fucking Hollywood. I taught Susan Faludi's last book in my seminar, but she lost her edge. I think she's fucking guys now. Although Ryanne Eisler's stuff still holds up, I haven't seen any new powerful revolutionary voices. It's all trash. Instead of an army of pissed-off women ready to wage war against the Man, we've been overrun by Lilith Fair feminists and lipstick lesbian sorority girls, who sell us out and switch over to the other side to become a slave to the cock and conformity by getting married. That's all we need, another fucking part-time lesbian turned breeder!"

Ivan was not familiar with any of the names, but he remembered about the lost book in his glove compartment. He idled his cab at a traffic light, then opened his glove compartment and removed a copy of *Gysana*.

"Do you want this book?" said Ivan.

The girly lesbian snatched the book out of Ivan's hand.

"Holy shit!" yelled the militant dyke.

"You know this book?" Ivan said.

"Of course!" they screamed in unison.

"I totally forgot about Mona LaVigne," said the girly lesbian. "She kicks ass! I think she's French-Canadian. Wow, this is her first novel. I used to jerk off to it when I read it in high school. The movie totally sucked, and I hated Katie Holmes in it. But my God, Jamie Lee Curtis has an amazing body."

"I'd fuck Jamie Lee Big Tits for sure!" the militant dyke said.

"I know the critics slammed her second novel *Squeeze Monkey*, but I liked it. She wrote that while living in Paris with her husband. I forget his name. Tenzin something or other. He's a writer too, a war correspondent. I think he died covering the civil war in Nepal."

"I never read her last novel," said the militant dyke.

"I did. The critics panned *Why I Don't Fuck Girls Anymore*. I don't know why they all of a sudden turned against her. OK, so with the exception of Mona LaVigne, there's no other revolutionary female writers in America."

"And she's fucking French-Canadian."

"You want the book?" Ivan said.

"Sure. I don't have a copy anymore," the girly lesbian answered. "Thanks. That's nice of you."

"He just wants to fuck you, Betty. Stop being so fucking grateful. Men don't give girls books unless they want to fuck them. It's the subtler, yet sophisticated approach that men use to feign intelligence. Most guys pick up slutty women in bars by pouring free drinks down their throats, but some perverts use books to lure women into bed, especially dirty books like anything from Henry Miller, Anais Nin, and the Marquis de Sade. Oh, and don't forget some Emily Dickinson poems."

"I didn't know about that," said the girly lesbian.

"Why would you? You are from fucking Idaho!"

The girly lesbian sighed. "Wyoming, not Idaho."

"The same fucking difference," the militant dyke said then howled like a dog. "All of you farm girls with literary aspirations flock to the city because you think you're going to find true love and become a famous novelist. They've been brainwashed by all of that subversive bullshit they see on *Sex in the City*."

"Uh oh. Please spare me another *Sex in the City* rant."

Ivan grew more curious once he heard *Sex in the City*. Olga and her mother watched it all the time. Ivan actually liked it, especially Charlotte. She made him horny and inspired numerous masturbation fantasies.

"*Sex in the City* brainwashed women. Instead of focusing on sexual empowerment, the show has become a commercial for the fashion industry. Instead of transforming the viewers into staunch feminists, the opposite happened and they became hyper-consumers. Many aspects of the feminist movement in the 1960s were nothing more than a carefully-concocted conspiracy by the male-dominated media to loosen up the social mores that society imposed upon women in the 1950s during post-World War II Americana. Many young women were raised by uptight parents who sheltered their sexuality. The feminist movement encouraged teenagers to rebel against the status quo. While some fought for equal rights and equal pay, the majority of women also discarded monogamy, thereby permitting men to go around and fuck whoever they wanted. Then the pharmaceutical companies got involved and created an evil pill for profit that allowed women to fuck as much as they desired without any risk of pregnancy. The medical community tricked us into manipulating our natural cycles with birth control pills. The man's evil pills allowed him to screw us all he wants at will without having to bear the responsibility of raising children. All of that free-loving hippie bullshit deceived women who thought they were empowering themselves by taking their sexuality into their own hands; instead they gave it right back by blowing any long hair who used Bob Dylan quotes to sum up life's little idiosyncrasies."

"You need to save these rants for your lectures," replied the girly lesbian.

The militant dyke rolled down her window and stuck her head outside the window. She shouted to no one in particular.

"Look around people. It's happening all over again. Britney Fucking Spears? Hello! Ooops! Fuck me one more time because I'm a Virgin! Hell yeah, if I ever come across Britney Spears, I'm gonna violate her with the 14-inch strap on and pull out all of her dyed-blonde hair extensions. Oh man, I could bite out her eyeballs and shove them up her cunt!"

The girly lesbian tried to pull her girlfriend back into the cab. She succeeded, but the bull dyke continued with her tirade.

"Britney and the rest of those pretty bitches singing bubblegum pop crap are whores who make record company suits billions of dollars. Their images grace magazine covers, billboards, and are splashed all over MTV. Britney is being used by the suits to brainwash teenagers all over America. Horny little boys see the videos and her fake tits and all they want to do is fuck her, and all those teenage girls see how the boys react, so they want to be desired just like that, so they dress like Britney and act like Britney and fuck like Britney Spears because they think that attention from boys is all that matters in this world. Boys are boys and if they don't fuck each other, they will fuck you for two or three minutes no matter what you fucking look like!"

Ivan laughed. She was right.

"And those fuckers at *Sex in the City* are just as culpable. They turned an entire generation of women into promiscuous consumers thereby eradicating any ground the feminist movement made during the 1970s and 80s. Now, we're all doomed to live under the shadow of a penis for the rest of eternity. Fucking kill me now."

The girly lesbian laughed and added, "You're so right. I mean, all those clothes they wear on the show or a cute purse one of them carries in a short scene is all part of a ploy to prey on weak women who want to look cool, so they'll sell out their individuality for a sense of materialistic style."

"And don't forget the fucking part," interrupted the dyke. "How many men do those sluts have sex with? I mean, that's just unreal. I laugh when I hear critics say that the show is innovative because it honestly depicts how women talk and really are. Hello! Most of the women I know aren't sluts and fashion whores. They do not want a boyfriend and they don't want to shop all the fucking time. But this fucking show is telling those younger women out there, 'Look if you don't want to die an old maid, then start chugging cock, buy better clothes and makeup, and if you sleep with enough guys, you'll find Mr. Big.'"

Ivan reached Park Slope and while they paid him the fare, he blurted something out.

"You know a lot about a TV show that you hate."

The militant dyke glared at Ivan, almost as if to challenge him to a fight.

"Yeah, I said that I hate fucking *Sex in the City*, but I never said I didn't watch it! I wouldn't miss it for the world. So, fuck you pig!"

Chapter 18

Ivan parked his cab three blocks from his apartment. He looked at the clock. 6:53 p.m. He had less than half an hour to take a dump, eat a sandwich, and jerk off. He called Kelly but she didn't answer. Ivan assumed she was at work, waitressing at a bistro in the West Village.

Kelly left Brooklyn after high school and moved into a NYU dormitory near Union Square. She had an inconsistent freshman year because she held multiple part-time jobs that sucked up all of her free time. Even with a juicy financial aid package, Kelly's living expenses were too high, so she worked two nights a week as a phone sex operator and four nights at Barnes and Noble on the north side of Union Square.

The bass player in Jack Tripper Stole My Dog, Kelly's boyfriend's band, invented a scam to steal expensive art books from Barnes and Noble and sell them at The Strand, which paid cash for high-quality used books. As a cashier, Kelly became an integral part of the theft ring. Different members of the band selected pricey art books and something from the discount bin. They brought all of the items up to the register, but Kelly only rang up the cheapest item. She then demagnetized the security tags hidden in the books' binding, in order to prevent the alarm from going off when they exited the store. For less than $10, the thieves pilfered $100 worth of books. They fenced the books down the street and used the proceeds to buy marijuana and mushrooms.

This scam worked for a few months and Kelly thought it was foolproof, until one of the managers noticed a pattern and set up a sting. Ken Murphy easily busted Kelly and even showed her the evidence. Murphy, an unattractive forty-something with bad breath, looked like a pedophile and often leered at young customers. He developed a crush on Kelly the moment she started working there. Murphy promised he wouldn't press charges if Kelly sucked him off. When she refused, he picked up the phone and dialed 9-1-1. Kelly begged him to hang up the phone and reluctantly agreed to service her boss in exchange for her freedom. Kelly agreed to meet Murphy at his apartment.

Kelly didn't want to tell her boyfriend what happened, because he'd beat the shit out of her if he found out that she fucked up. She definitely didn't want to tell Ivan, who had grown increasingly jealous ever since she began dating the lead guitar player from Jack Tripper Stole My Dog. Like most of her problems, Kelly kept them to herself. She returned to her dorm room, downed seven shots of vodka (chased with a warm can of Diet Coke), and smoked a joint before she hopped on the subway.

Kelly almost chickened out after she had panic attack on the subway. She composed herself and continued on with the plan. Murphy lived in the basement of his mother's house in Queens. He wore only a bathrobe when he answered the door. Kelly walked inside and he bolted the front door. Kelly didn't waste any time. She kneeled down in front of him, and stroked his pencil-thin uncircumcised penis. The smells emanating from his crotch almost made her puke. She held her nose and slid his penis into her mouth.

"Don't think about it," Kelly reminded herself. "Get it over with as quickly as possible. This is just a small price to pay for stealing thousands of dollars worth of books."

Murphy's awkward sexual experiences only included prostitutes he hired from ads in the back of the Village Voice. He couldn't control himself and ejaculated less than ten seconds into the blowjob. Kelly initially gagged. She tried to pull away, but Murphy grabbed her head and didn't let go until he finished.

Kelly choked and coughed up Murphy's semen on her palm. Murphy felt ashamed at his lack of stamina, but his embarrassment morphed into rage. He slapped Kelly across the face.

"Swallow that right now!"

He slapped her again and tears trickled down her face. He slapped her a third time and she sloppily slurped up a white glob. Kelly stood up and rushed toward the door, but Murphy grabbed her arm and twisted it behind her back. She screamed, but he quickly silenced her by stuffing a soiled sock in her mouth, ensuring that his mother wouldn't hear her pleas for help. He dragged her into his bedroom and assaulted her for two hours before she managed to escape.

Kelly didn't know what to do. If she reported Murphy to the cops, then Barnes and Noble would press charges and she'd get thrown in jail, along with her boyfriend and everyone else from Jack Tripper Stole My Dog. When she told her boyfriend about getting busted, he instantly flew into a fit of rage. He blamed Kelly for the entire situation. He insisted that if she didn't fuck up, then Murphy's molestation wouldn't have happened. In his twisted mind, Kelly got what she deserved.

A confused Kelly wanted to tell Ivan, because he'd want to exact revenge on Murphy without involving the police. She was about to tell Ivan about everything, but then 9/11 happened. Her father went missing and everything in her world slowed down. She faded away into the land of denial.

Ivan lived in a railroad-style apartment in a building owned by Pytor. Ivan, Olga, and Olga's mother lived in one of the two apartments on the top story of a five-floor building. A yuppie couple moved in across the hall. They never fought, ordered in a lot of food, and had very loud sex twice a week like clockwork on Saturdays and Wednesdays.

Ivan was excited to shit on his own throne. He often had to use a filthy public toilet somewhere in the city. Ivan opened the door and the Old Mule had fallen asleep on the couch. Ivan could hear Olga's mother snoring from down the hall. He snuck past her and rushed into the bathroom.

After he flushed the toilet, he heard a suspicious noise that was not associated with snoring. Olga normally worked until nine or ten on Saturdays, so he did not expect to see anyone else at home. He walked into the hallway and spotted a t-shirt that did not belong to him. He heard more noises emanating from his bedroom. The door was always left open, but that time it was closed. He put his ear against the door and heard the familiar slapping and grunting sounds associated with intercourse. He slowly opened the door and peeked inside. Olga's head was buried underneath a pillow while a skinny man stood alongside the bed and fucked her doggie style. She used the pillow to muffle her screams, while the skinny fellow held on to her for dear life.

Ivan quietly shut the door. He recognized the skinny guy – Alexi the dispatcher from Pytor's limo company. Alexi hooked Ivan up with his pink speed pills, but the entire time he was also fucking his wife.

Ivan did not know how to react. The Ecstasy squashed any urges toward violence, so the love drug that he accidently ingested had actually saved Alexi from the beating of his life. Ivan took a couple of deep breaths and exited the apartment. He opened up the door to his cab and sat down. He knew he had no right to be angry because he constantly cheated on Olga. They were not married for more than a month before he began the first of over a dozen affairs, not including visits to assorted tranny hookers that he picked up on Tenth Avenue. Olga didn't have a clue about any of the affairs, nor did she suspect Ivan's ongoing relationship with Kelly.

Even for an unattractive cab driver, Ivan got lucky more than once by simply being at the right place at the right time. That time usually occurred when bars closed and a horde of drunks stumbled onto the streets of Manhattan between 3 and 4 a.m. That was one of the main reasons why Ivan preferred the night shift – for a shot at picking up a lonely, intoxicated woman who desperately needed some long-dicking. They were easy targets, but they rarely called back because they were too embarrassed they slept with a balding cabbie with a lumpy head.

Chapter 19

On his way into Manhattan, Ivan picked up a fare headed to a bar near NYU. The law student talked on his phone the entire ride, mostly about somebody named Ed who was having sex with his sister's boyfriend, but she didn't know that her boyfriend was gay, and it blew up into a huge scandal for their provincial Ohio town.

Ivan drove over the Manhattan Bridge and could not stop thinking about Olga. They only got married because she was pregnant with Sasha. Ivan finally developed a routine where he drove a cab in Pytor's fleet at night and painted apartments during the day. That's when he met Olga – he had painted her apartment. He took her out on a few dates and she got knocked up rather quickly. He did not want a wife, nor another child. He was already estranged from his son and ex-wife Misha. Another child would complicate things. He wanted to enjoy the freedoms of being single in New York City. But somehow, Olga tricked him into marrying her.

Ivan analyzed their 20-year loveless marriage and came to the conclusion that he had been a horrible husband and an even worse father. It was easy to blame Olga for all his problems, and vice versa. Instead of taking responsibility for their own lives, they passed the blame onto each other. Olga's affair with Alexi made perfect sense because Ivan was never in love with her, nor did he ever display any affection. Even money-grubbing alcoholic cows needed love too. No wonder she hated him.

Alexi was a handsome young man and could be with any woman he wanted. But what made Olga attractive to him? Olga looked like a state penitentiary prison guard with warts that covered her hands and knuckles. Maybe that was his type? It began to make more sense that Alexi and Olga were fuck buddies. He always asked innocent questions about Olga, small talk mostly, but Ivan brushed it aside as if someone were bullshitting about the weather or asking about the final score of the Yankees game.

That's when Ivan recalled two instances when he found Alexi hanging out at his apartment. Ivan assumed that Alexi was one of those dealers who made house calls to sell him speed. It never occurred to him that Alexi had just banged Olga. Ivan should have recognized all the signs, but he was too concerned with his own affair and thereby failed to connect the dots. His primary focus was covering up any links to Kelly.

Before Kelly dropped out of college, Ivan often snuck into her dorm room for romps. Kelly's roommate pretended to be asleep, but she heard everything, even though she pulled the covers over her ears to block out the sounds of Kelly's screams during marathon Viagra-induced sessions. Kelly often made strange sounds that imitated two wounded raccoons biting each others' tails, which often woke up the entire dorm. Some of Kelly's neighbors gathered outside her door and recorded the dying raccoon sounds.

Ivan dropped off his fare in front of a bar on MacDougal Street. He looked at the clock. 7:59 p.m. He heard a knock on his window. An Asian man with a video camera stood next to a young black woman with a clipboard. Ivan knew right away that they were NYU film students before they offered to show him their IDs.

"Excuse me, sir, my name is Annie and this is Tim and we are grad students. We wanted to talk to a taxi driver as part of our documentary film. Are you interested?"

She handed Ivan a copy of their film assignment and a waiver allowing them to use his image. Ivan suffered from dyslexia and had a tough time reading English. He barely glanced at the paper and handed it back to the grad student.

"It's a documentary about the functioning systems of our society, and how they reflect our culture and our future. We wanted to interview a couple of different people who worked in the field of transportation."

Ivan thought for a few moments. At least once every six months or so, different film crews approached him with similar requests. Every young filmmaker who moved to New York City yearned to do a documentary on street life, and many of them ended up asking Ivan for an interview. Ivan always turned them down, but the Ecstasy encouraged him to open up. Every half hour or so, waves of euphoria attacked Ivan's senses. He grew instantly attached to his passengers, intimately connected to their lives. During those same moments, he was working and they were living, but they still shared a similar experience on their life's journey.

"I must be interesting," thought Ivan, if he was constantly approached by different filmmakers. Why would they waste their time and money shooting a movie about someone who was ordinarily boring? Delusions of grandeur set in and Ivan talked himself into doing the documentary. He thought the film would help him launch a career in Hollywood. When TV execs saw the film, they'd all fight over which one of them got to sign Ivan to a multi-million dollar contract to produce his own reality show – *Ivan the Russian Cab Driver*. He'd become a huge star, just like Ozzy Osbourne and Anna Nicole Smith. Once he became famous, he could finally divorce Olga and marry Kelly. The two of them would move to Los Angeles, where Ivan would start a limousine company that drove around rich celebrities to clubs, film premieres, and cocaine-infused after-parties.

"Do I get paid?" blurted out Ivan.

"Not at all," said Tim. "We're poor students. This is art. Don't you want to help support the arts?"

"No."

Ivan changed his mind, but Annie worked out a compromise. Ivan agreed to drive around for 15 to 20 minutes with the camera rolling. While he drove around, Annie would ask him a series of questions. When their time was up, they'd stop filming and pay him whatever amount appeared on the meter.

"Plus a $5 tip," Ivan sternly negotiated.

Chapter 20

Annie sat in the back seat and Tim the cameraman sat in the front. Ivan leisurely drove north on Sixth Avenue and Tim began shooting.

"We'll start out slow with simple biographical questions to let you get comfortable before we get into more serious stuff. So, what's your name and where are you from?"

"I am Ivan from Brooklyn," he proudly stated.

"Where were you born."

"Moscow."

"What did you do in Russia before you came to America?"

"Soldier."

"Army?"

"The Red Army."

"Did you join?"

"Drafted. Afghanistan War."

"Wow, so you fought against the Taliban?"

"Taliban not exist yet."

"So who did you fight?"

"Rebels. Your CIA gave money to Osama Bin Laden. Osama trained rebels. Russia left Afghanistan and the rebels became Taliban."

"So you're saying that the CIA created the Taliban?"

"Yes."

"How long were you in Afghanistan?"

"Eight months before I got sent home."

"Why did they send you home?"

"My unit got ambushed."

"Did you get injured?"

"Yes."

"Wow, I'm sorry."

"I'm lucky."

"Why do you say that?"

"My friends returned to Russia in body bags."

"Did you get a Purple Heart?"

"Saint George Cross."

"Was that for bravery?"

"For not dying."

"Do you still have the medal?"

"Sold it."

"For?"

"Record."

"Which one?"

"Johnny Cash."

"No shit?"

"Yes."

"You like Johnny Cash?"

"Yes. Want to listen?"

Ivan removed Johnny Cash's *Greatest Hits* from the glove compartment and slid the disc into his CD player. The opening notes to "Jackson" began to play.

"And what did you do after the war?"

"I got married. Moved to Leningrad."

"What did you do there?"

"Factory."

"So when did you come to America?"

"When my wife and son left me."

"They left you? Why did they leave?"

"I had affair with boss's wife and his daughter."

"What?"

"Yes."

"Wow, so I'm assuming your wife caught you?"

"Yes."

"I'm sorry."

"I'm not. I did not love her. I was in love with her sister."

"Her sister? Why didn't you marry her sister?"

"Suicide."

"She killed herself?"

"Jumped off a building."

"I'm sorry."

"Me too."

"Ummm, maybe we should change the subject. Ummm, so when did you come to America?"

"1982."

"How did you become a cab driver?"

"Yuri, my brother, got me the job."

"Who was the most famous person you ever drove?"

"Tom Brokaw. News guy. Good tipper."

"Wow, Brokaw. Anyone else?"

"Tony Randall."

"From *The Odd Couple*?"

"Yes. That asshole stiffed me."

Annie and Tim both laughed.

"What is the worst part about driving a cab?"

"When disrespectful passengers treat me like shit."

"Do you hate traffic?"

"No. I really hate cleaning the back seat. Every night it's the same. Puke. Piss. Shit. Blood. Cum."

Annie quickly scanned the back seat to make sure she wasn't sitting in bodily fluids before she continued. "So, I have to assume that people have had sex in your cab?"

"Yes."

"Do they tip?"

"Average tippers. But the gay businessmen tip me best."

"Gay businessmen?"

"Yes. They use backseat for quickie blowjobs."

"Does gay sex bother you?"

"No. I'm not gay, but sometimes, I like to watch."

That response elicited giggles from Annie and Tim.

"So, how did you learn English?"

"*Dukes of Hazzard* and *M*A*S*H*."

"From TV?"

"Yes."

"Do you like America better than Russia?"

"Yes."

"Why?"

"Because you can leave."

"What don't you like about America?"

"People who complain about this country and say 'Fuck America' and 'Fuck George Bush,' but I want to tell them, 'If you don't like America, then leave!'"

"That's an interesting attitude."

"My unhappy wife wants to go back home to the Ukraine. So I tell her, 'Go back to the farm, you pig!'"

Both Annie and Tim laughed again.

"You laugh now, but it sounds funnier in Russian."

"So, Ivan, I assume that you're married again?"

"Yes."

"How long?"

"Too long."

"Did you have any children together?"

"Daughter."

"What does your daughter do?"

"Lesbians."

"I'm sorry?"

"Lesbians."

"She likes girls?"

"Yes. She used to sleep with my girlfriend."

"Wait a sec... did you say girlfriend?"

"Yes."

"So, you have a wife and a girlfriend?"

"Yes."

"Let me get this straight. Your current girlfriend used to sleep with your daughter."

"They're best friends."

"So you're sleeping with your daughter's best friend? Does your daughter know?"

"No."

"That is unreal. And your wife has no idea?"

"I don't know. She's having an affair too."

"Oh my God, this sounds like a Jerry Springer episode."

"This… is my life."

Chapter 21

Ivan drove around the West Village for almost twenty minutes. He circled back to Washington Square Park and dropped off Annie and Tim. The film students thanked him, paid him for his time and asked him for his email address. Ivan scribbled down – IvanElvis69@aol.com.

Ivan pulled away, but forgot to tell Annie about the only other time he participated in a film. Two years earlier, Ivan made his auspicious debut in a porno flick. At a hotel in Soho, Ivan picked up an unusual married couple – a heavyset middle-aged guy and a short Asian woman. The passengers never gave Ivan a specific destination. Instead, the fat man said, "Just drive around for a while. My wife has never been to New York before."

The Thai girl pulled a video camera out of an oversized pink purse. She rolled down the window and began recording as Ivan drove through Chinatown.

The fat man had very friendly eyes and wore a lot of jewelry. Ivan presumed he was rich, because that was the only reason why hot women married fat guys. Money. Ivan could not stop staring at the woman because she had the biggest fake breasts he had ever seen on an Asian girl.

After a few minutes of small talk, the fat man told Ivan that his wife was originally from Thailand, but they had met at a gym in North Hollywood. Ivan was skeptical because fat men did not work out. He suspected she was actually a mail-order bride.

The man handed Ivan his business card, which read:

Peter Carini

President

Backseat Productions

Chatsworth, CA

"I want to hire you to drive us around for the afternoon," Carini said. "How much do you usually make an hour?"

"$100," Ivan lied. It was more like $45.

"Sounds good to me."

Ivan turned off the meter and agreed to drive the couple around Manhattan for $100/hour. It sounded too good to be true, and that's when things took an abrupt turn. Ivan glanced into the rearview mirror and watched as the Thai girl's head bobbed up and down. Carini clutched the camera with one hand and alternated shots between his wife licking his love pump and whatever famous landmark Ivan passed at the time.

Over an hour went by and Carini asked Ivan if he wanted to participate as a cameraman. He parked the cab on Tenth Avenue in Hell's Kitchen and Carini handed over the camera. Ivan remained in the front of the cab, but sat sideways in the passenger seat to film the completely naked couple. Carini mounted the Thai girl in the missionary position, before they switched to doggie style. A few pedestrians passed by the cab, but they hardly noticed the porn movie being filmed in the backseat.

Ivan's shooting skills impressed Carini, particularly a magnificent close up of the Thai girl's snatch revealing a cream pie. Ivan appreciated the compliment and felt like the Woody Allen of gonzo porn.

"So, do you wanna act in one scene?"

Ivan couldn't believe his luck. He was already having the best day he ever had as a cab driver, but to top it all off, Carini gave him a chance to have his cock sucked by an actual porn star. Ivan jumped out of the cab and switched places with Carini. Ivan slid into the backseat and played with the Thai girl's fake breasts like he was a boxer practicing with a speed bag. She massaged his bald head and stroked his crotch.

The Thai girl unzipped Ivan's pants and gasped. She was flabbergasted at the overall length and girth of his penis. As a six-year veteran of the adult entertainment industry, the Thai girl had never seen anything like it.

"It's bigger than my arm!" she squealed.

"For God's sake Ivan, that thing is a fucking monster. You should move out to California and I'll make you a huge star."

Ivan was more embarrassed than proud. He always knew that he was well-endowed, but he never considered a career in the porn industry. The Thai girl reached into her bag and pulled out a black dildo. She asked Ivan if she could stick it in his butt. He didn't know what to say, but she never waited for an answer. She inserted the tip of her dildo into his anus and rotated counter-clockwise until more than half of it disappeared. She stroked Ivan's penis for a few minutes with a pensive gaze. She was legitimately trying to figure out how to attack it. She initially struggled to wrap her tiny mouth around his penis, yet she still miraculously swallowed two-thirds of his shaft without choking to death.

"Whatever you do, Ivan, don't come in her mouth!" screamed Carini. "Make sure you pull out and come on her face. That's the money shot!"

Ivan followed Carini's directions and ejaculated on the side of the Thai girl's face. Semen landed on her neck and dripped onto her mountainous breasts. She rubbed Ivan's goo all over the peaks and valleys of her chest and then shoved her sticky fingers into his mouth.

"Does it taste good?" cooed the Thai girl.

"Tastes like vodka," mumbled Ivan as he plucked the dildo out of his ass.

Carini wanted to film one more scene and Ivan obliged. The Thai girl climbed on top in the reverse cowgirl position. She rode Ivan for about fifteen minutes, then begged to stop after she climaxed a second time.

"My pussy is going to hurt for a week," she joked.

After renting out his cab for almost four hours, Carini paid Ivan $500 in cash, including a $100 tip. To date, that was the biggest tip Ivan ever received, topping a $90 tip a wiseguy from Vinny the Chin's crew once gave Ivan for an impromptu trip to Atlantic City.

Ivan's blowjob scene appeared in *Misty Rain's Money Shots 7: I Heart NY*. He never saw the film, nor did he receive any royalties. In the closing credits, Ivan was listed as "Ivan Smirnoff."

Unknown to Ivan, the video became a huge success overseas. His infamous scene with the Thai girl garnered an award for "Best Blowjob" by Kuchi Kuchi, the most popular porn magazine in Japan. The editor also nicknamed Ivan, "Hiro Sinchawa Cocksumi," which loosely translated as "lumpy-headed man with a monster penis."

Chapter 22

"93rd and West End," said an average-looking thirty-something white guy as he violently slammed the door.

Ivan nodded.

"Life sucks... sometimes."

"All the time," shot back Ivan.

"Fucking right," agreed the average guy "Life sucks all the time. I can't fucking do anything right. Everyone hates me at work, but I don't know why because I'm the one pulling in the most business in the firm while everyone else fucks off all day dicking around on MySpace or IMing each other. It sucks that I get a paltry commission considering I generate enough sales revenue every quarter to pay everyone's salary. And do they ever thank me? No. Ungrateful assholes. Instead, they scurry out of the office as soon the clock strikes five, just like Fred Fucking Flintstone. They're out getting hammered at Happy Hour, while I'm staying late every night making phone calls. My boss is a fucking cocksucker too, because he's got no respect for my ability to close deals. That parasite never lifts a finger to help me out with clients so I get stuck with all the heavy lifting. As the head of our department, he's the one who gets all the accolades from the CEO, including a fat year-end bonus that's worth more than my base pay. That scumbag won't promote me because then he'll lose his top earner. I don't know why I keep being his bitch. One day I'll grow a pair of balls and tell him to fuck off. Maybe I should rat him out to H.R., because he's constantly trying to bang every piece of ass in our office, which means that I've been passed over for a promotion four times in the last three years, every time by a woman he was coincidentally trying to bang. None of them had my stellar qualifications, except that they had three holes and two tits and that's all that matters these days. The sad part of the story is that my boss is so fucking lame he never slept with any of them! I have to give those girls credit; they were smart enough to know they didn't have to give it up to get promoted. My boss is such a stupid schmuck. He totally got played. A real genius would have figured out a way to bang all of them before he handed out a promotion. I work for inbred twats."

Ivan often acted as a therapist when his passengers had a bad day. The ones who got the most off their chests felt relieved when the ride was over, and as a result, they felt obligated to tip Ivan a few extra dollars for listening to them vent.

"I don't know why some of these women fall for the biggest douchebags on the planet. I mean, it's like high school all fucking over again. Am I not smart enough? I have two graduate degrees, and one of them from an Ivy League school. The last girl I dated dumped me because she said I didn't make enough money. I mean, I'm not super rich, but I'm not poor either. I make 200K a year as a base salary not including commission and bonuses. How many people in the city make at least a quarter mil a year? It's gotta be less than 5%, right? I'm more successful than 95% of the rest of the schmucks out there, but that gold-digger wanted more. You know what? Fuck her. Let her find some hedge fund asshole to pay for her fucking summer house in the Hamptons. I don't fucking know what's wrong with me. I can't find anyone what wants to even sit down and have a meal with me, let alone suck my dick. You're never good enough in this town, because someone is always better. No matter how hard you try, I'm never good enough. And if by chance I happen to meet someone cool? She always has a boyfriend. Or worse? She doesn't have a boyfriend, but just wants to be friends. I'm never a lover or a boyfriend. I'm always just a fucking friend."

Ivan felt sorry for the average-looking white guy. If Sasha wasn't a lesbian, he would've considered setting her up.

"Money doesn't solve anything. I make money and I'm fucking miserable. You're a cab driver. You see people every fucking day. Doesn't it seem as though the richest people in the city are actually the most troubled?"

Ivan nodded.

"I see the looks on their faces," continued the average white guy. "They're zombies. Fucking stiffs. And the rest of them who aren't zombies? They are really good actors. It's a charade. A fucking scam. They keep up the ruse out of sheer fear because if they walked away from it, that would invalidate their lives. And all that hard work would have been for nothing. What's the point of waking up to live a life that's not your own? People wake up, shower, get dressed, and put on their masks before they walk outside into the real world. They walk around the office all day in a disguise. I do it every day. I should get an Oscar for my award-winning performance as a suit. Why do I do it? I'm afraid. Just like everyone else. I'm too chickenshit to walk up to my boss and tell him that he's a fucking asshole. I'm too afraid to quit. I won't. I can't. Wearing the mask is addictive. It's like a drug, stronger than heroin. It kills all the pain because when you wear a mask, you don't reveal your true self to the world, which means you don't get hurt. Everyone wants to belong and fit in, so they become an acceptable archetype to avoid the fear of rejection. They play it safe instead of living life. This so-called great American society puts too much pressure on its citizens to conform into these ideal clones that do nothing except borrow money in order to buy shit they think will make them look cool, or help distract them from discovering the truths about the world – how we've all been castrated into docile lemmings. A few people crack up and go crazy when they're unable to conform. That's why there's all those high school shootings, or why mailmen go postal and shoot up their co-workers. With the exception of oil and cocaine, this country has an overabundance of almost everything you can imagine. Yet, we've developed into a nation of generic, interchangeable, uncreative sheep. We allowed ourselves to become slaves to the Man, who controlled us with our own fears. It's so fucking bad you can feel fear, see fear, smell fear, and taste fear."

"Hmmm, taste the fear," Ivan blurted out.

"Taste the fucking fear! And it's gotten worse after 9/11. Look, I'm not one of those fucking crackpot conspiracy theorists who think that Dick Cheney blew up the Twin Towers with his cell phone, but you have to admit that the entire country has been cowering in fear since it happened. Now it's widespread fear. Dirty bomb fear. Anthrax fear. Sniper fear. Al-Qaeda fear. All the TV news networks and newspapers do is fear monger all day and night, while the politicians wave the bloody fucking flag to encourage us to bomb the fuck out of a bunch of Arabs on the other side of the planet. Am I the only one who realizes this? I mean, even my mother got brainwashed and she's a bona fide hippie who went to Woodstock. I was probably conceived in the middle of Max Yasgur's farm. She was the most open-minded, tolerant person in the world, but all that fear mongering got to her. When she visited me in the city for Mother's Day, she wouldn't tip the cab driver because he was an Arab. When I prodded her about it, she admitted she was reluctant to give any cabbies money because they would turn around and hand the money over to Osama Bin Laden. Do you fucking believe that? They did such a good job instilling fear into everyone's psyche that they scared the shit out of my mother. In a single day, they turned a bleeding heart into a callous xenophobe."

Chapter 23

"They're all crazy," said the guy who looked like Page 34 of the J. Crew summer catalogue.

"But you have to find the one who is the least crazy," replied his perfectly coiffed friend, who resembled the J. Crew model on Page 41.

Ivan had picked up a couple of frat boys in front of a bar on Columbus Avenue. They requested a bar he'd never heard of in Murray Hill.

"Most of the women I know are completely insane," said Page 34. "Especially in this city, they are all crazy. Every single woman I meet is fucked up because of their parents or something their last boyfriend did to them. I mean, when I first meet a girl, they do a great job at hiding their insanity until one day, she flips a switch and turns into a psychopath. I'm telling you. All women are crazy."

Ivan did a quick inventory in his head. His mother? Crazy and insane. The old lady who molested him when he was a kid? Insane and crazy. Petra? Mad and insane. Misha? Crazy. Olga? Extremely crazy and a bad drunk. Sasha? Extremely crazy, just like her mother. And Kelly? Crazy, but a cute crazy.

"Did you ever think that maybe sometimes, it's not their fault?" said Page 41. "Sometimes, things happen in people's lives that they have no control over, which affects them for the rest of eternity. Men do pretty bad things to women and say bad things to them, so maybe that's part of the reason why they go crazy."

"Yeah, but this woman in my office? She's just fucking nuts. I didn't know why I never listened to my father. He always said, 'Don't shit where you eat.' I never understood what he meant until now. I should've taken his advice. Never shit where you eat."

"I don't get it."

"You know, don't dip your pen in company ink. Don't sleep with anyone you work with. Don't shit where you eat."

"Wait, so you slept with someone from your office? Who? Was it that hottie half-Japanese, half-Jewish chick?"

"I wish. I made the mistake of asking out the Sad Girl."

"Sad Girl?"

"Yeah, there's this girl in the office that we make fun of. She's the Sad Girl and always looks like her cat just died. She never smiles. She always looks like she's gonna cry. Don't you have one of those?"

"At Deutsche Bank? Almost everyone there is. And the Germans I work for? They all look like their cat just died."

"Well, mostly everyone in my office is a lot more cheery than those dreary Germans. I think it's because there's a Starbucks in our lobby. Anyway, during the Fourth of July my assistant, Jess, threw a housewarming party. She and her fiancé had just moved into a cool apartment in Hell's Kitchen with access to a roof deck and everything. So she invited a bunch of people from work. I had gone to the Yanks game that afternoon with Smitty and we got crocked. When the game ended, Smitty went across the street and drank at the bowling alley for a couple of hours. So now you know I was good and toasty before I finally made my way to Hell's Kitchen. I wasn't even at the party for like five minutes before I got cornered by Annoying Guy."

"Annoying Guy?"

"Yeah, Annoying Guy. Every office has one, that guy who walks around all day and bugs the shit out of everyone. Well, I got stuck talking to Annoying Guy, when I saw Sad Girl leaning up against the wall. A sad wallflower. I never really talked to her much, but I was so happy to see her because she was my only out. I kinda called out to her and when she looked up, I excused myself and broke free from Annoying Guy. So, we started chatting and found out that we had some common musical interests. I had to take a piss so I went to the bathroom, but there was a line, so I bullshitted with one of the kids from the IT department. He mentioned that he had some blow and offered me a bump. We must've been in the bathroom for like twenty minutes because everyone kept banging on the door, while we ripped biker rails. It was some good shit too. Made my nose and lips numb. We finally left the bathroom and went up to the roof, because I hadn't seen it yet. The kid from the IT department introduced me to his girlfriend. The first thing she said was, 'Do you wanna buy some E?'"

"What? No way."

"True story. That's what she did… she was dealing E. So I didn't think twice. I whipped out a $20 bill and she gave me an orange pill with the Mitsubishi logo on it."

"Like the Japanese car company."

"Exactly like it. Not only was I drunk and coked up, I was also a fucking lit monkey because of the E. So I'm running my mouth saying who the fuck knows what and I'm jumping up and down when the fireworks went off, and I was hugging everyone, even Annoying Guy and Sad Girl."

"Uh oh. I see where this is going."

"I don't know how it happened, but Sad Girl and I left the party at the same time so I offered to split a cab. We weren't even in the backseat for five seconds and we were making out. I mean, I was so wasted that I'd be kissing a giraffe. Shit, you'd be kissing a giraffe if you were half as fucked up as I was. One thing leads to another and she's got her hand in my pants giving me a hand job. When we got to her apartment, she invited me upstairs. We walked into her apartment and she practically raped me. I couldn't keep up with her. Every time we finished coming, she'd want to go again. I passed out eventually, but she must have woken me up two or three times during the night to have sex."

"Note to self," snarked Page 41. "Sad Girls are nymphomaniacs."

"When I woke up the next morning, I wanted to make things 100% clear between us, so I took Sad Girl to breakfast and told her I was a little too wasted and let things get carried away. I told her even though she was really nice, I wasn't interested in dating or anything. Then I gave her this long talk explaining how I'm still hopelessly in love with this painter that I dated during grad school until she moved to New Mexico for a while, and although we had broken up, she was now thinking about moving back to New York, and I wanted to allow our relationship to work itself out."

"So what did she say?"

"Sad Girl said she understood my point and wanted me as a friend. I thought everything was cool, until later that week I noticed she was acting really clingy at work. We went out to lunch one day and she freaked me out when she said 'If you ever meet anyone, please let me know.'"

"Whaaaa?"

"That's what I said! I was thinking to myself, 'Is this chick for real?' That's a deal that you make with someone if you're casually having sex with them, but not really dating. I told her, 'No dice.' I mean come on, what was I going to do if I met a hottie in a bar and she wanted to go home with me? Do I say, 'Hold up a second, I have to call Sad Girl, to make sure it's kosher that I take you home and eat your pussy.' Come on. That's absurd. I guess she didn't believe me when I told her about my ex-girlfriend from New Mexico."

"That's a little crazy. I lived with women who kept me on a looser leash!"

"Seriously. Anyway, by the end of the July, it had been at least three weeks since I slept with her, and she started stalking me. She started out on Stalker Level 1, which included walking past my cubicle twenty times a day, or constantly asking me if I had lunch plans. I don't know how she got my unlisted home number, but as soon as she acquired that info, she ascended to Stalker Level 2. She called me every night, but I never answered. Then one day, I went into the office, and one of my co-workers gave me shit about a picture of me on the wall of Sad Girl's cubicle. Someone at Jess' Fourth of July party took a bunch of photos, and there's was one photo of me hugging Sad Girl, while I was tripping balls on Ecstasy. At that point she jumped up to Stalker Level 4. That's when the calls to my home phone increased exponentially to like ten times a day. At the beginning of August, she randomly showed up at places I was going – like the Cedar Tavern, or Joshua Tree, or seeing John Scofield's band play at Bowery Ballroom.

"Let me guess... Stalker Level 5?"

"Yeah. Then it got really ugly. My assistant came into work one morning and congratulated me on going out with Sad Girl. She thought it was really sweet that we were dating and that we made a great couple. Apparently, a couple of the girls in the office went out the night before for Happy Hour and Sad Girl told everyone that we had been going out since the Fourth of July."

"What happened?"

"I was livid. I told Jess the truth about what happened. I could tell she was taken aback by it, but agreed that Sad Girl was way out of line."

"Did she confront Sad Girl?"

"I presume so, but I don't know for sure. Anyway, last weekend I went out to the Hamptons with Smitty. I left on Friday and got back Sunday afternoon. I wasn't even gone for 40 hours and she had called 83 times! But get this – she did not leave one message. I couldn't believe my Caller ID. It had 86 total calls. One was from my mother, two were telemarketers, and the other 83 were from Sad Girl. For a while she had been calling every hour on the hour. Then it got really crazy on Saturday after midnight because I noticed she had called me every nine minutes at one point. 12:21. 12:30. 12:39. 12:48. 12:57. 1:06. Jeez, if that wasn't enough, I also found out from my doorman that she had stopped by three times that weekend looking for me."

"Wow, that chick is out of control."

"When I got to work that Monday, Sad Girl was waiting for me in front of my cube. She made a huge fucking scene and called me an asshole for talking to her friends about our relationship behind her back, and I'm like, 'What fucking relationship? We hooked up once, that's it, end of story! You started stalking me and told everyone in the office we were dating, when it's not fucking true, so I asked Jess for advice.' I was about to suggest that we take the discussion elsewhere, but I was afraid that she was so crazy that she'd accuse me of assault or something. At that point she started crying and by then, everyone in the office had popped their heads out of their cubes to listen, like little hedgehogs, their heads popped up one-by-one. Jess discreetly called security and they took Sad Girl away. I spent the rest of the day in the H.R. department filling out an incident report. My boss was pretty disappointed with me, which sucked, because it wasn't even my fault."

"So what happened?"

"Well, that was on Monday. She never came back to work on Tuesday or Wednesday, or the rest of the week."

"Did she quit?"

"Nope. She drank an entire bottle of NyQuil and jumped off the back of the Staten Island Ferry. She's in Bellevue now after the harbor police fished her out."

"Holy shit."

"Like I said… all women are crazy."

Chapter 24

Ivan's last fare of the night, an intoxicated married couple, fought during the entire ride to Grand Central Station. Ivan remained silent and listened. The wife grew so furious she almost slugged her husband. Ivan anticipated a backseat brawl, but the two only exchanged a few more verbal barbs. They stiffed Ivan with a lousy tip and disappeared into the terminal.

Ivan flipped the switch on his "Off Duty" light. He had called Kelly four times, but she never answered. After an arduous Saturday in the concrete jungle, a depraved Ivan was thirsty for water and sex – both extreme side effects of the Ecstasy. While waiting at one traffic light, Ivan drank an entire bottle of water. He'd also driven around with an erection for most of his shift – with Kelly's name written all over it.

Ivan stopped by the Italian bistro in the West Village where Kelly worked, but he couldn't find her. One of the waiters said she wasn't feeling well and left several hours earlier. Ivan hopped back in his cab and turned down a couple of soused frat boys, who dangled a $20 tip in front of him in exchange for a ride to Jersey City. Ivan drove into Brooklyn over the Williamsburg Bridge, a route that he traversed a thousand times before. He could do it in his sleep or crocked on two liters of vodka.

A single candle illuminated the loft. Ivan could barely see Kelly's shadowy figure in the faint flicker of light. She was curled up in a ball on the bean bag. Ivan sat down on the edge of the couch and listened to Kelly's sniffling sounds as a raging river of tears threatened to burst through her fragile dam – her tightly shut eyes. She opened up one, then the other. Waterfalls ensued.

"Don't cry kitten," Ivan begged.

Ivan never handled emotional women very well. Crying repulsed him, but he tried to hug Kelly. Instead of melting in his arms, she wiggled out of his grip. A frustrated Ivan stormed off into the kitchen. He fumbled around the sink and found a somewhat-clean pint glass. He took the last two ice cubes from the tray and poured himself a large serving of vodka on ice. He grabbed a jar of peanut butter – the only edible item in the refrigerator – and rammed his index finger into the jar. He swirled it around and shoved a brownish glob into his mouth. He washed it down with the vodka.

"Please leave," Kelly whimpered.

Ivan wanted to sleep with Kelly while her boyfriend was on the road. That was their plan, but Kelly wasn't in the mood. He didn't know how to make things better, other than let her cry herself to sleep and return in the morning.

Kelly didn't want Ivan to leave. When she said "leave," she really meant "stay." Instead, she pushed him away. She wanted to tell him so many things face-to-face, but she was not brave enough to look him in the eye. She scribbled down all of her thoughts in a note, and hoped that if she grew too anxious, then she could read it to him.

Alas, she froze up when Ivan rang the bell. Opting for a non-confrontational tense moment, she rocked back and forth and repeatedly uttered, "Please leave. Please leave. Please. Leave. Leave. Leave. Please Leave. Leave. Leave. Now."

She should have stuck to the script and told Ivan everything.

"I love you, but I don't know if I'm in love with you. I have feelings for my boyfriend. I know he treats me like shit, but I need to be with someone my own age. If I want to be an actress,

I need to be with someone who inspires me. I don't care if his music sucks, it's not the point, because it's about how he makes me feel alive after he creates something from nothing. It causes a rush inside of me. I'm still in love with Sasha. Madly. She screwed me over. We were supposed to save up money and move to San Francisco together. I wanted Sasha. I wanted to move on with my life, but she bailed on me for another woman. And now I can't move on. I wanted to move far away from New York. Far away from the past. From the bad memories. From the dark memories. I needed to move away from my mother. Her denial is going to kill her. My father is dead and he's never coming home. We'll never find the body. He got pulverized when the towers fell. When will she give up? When can we finally have a funeral? It's been almost a year. I need the closure. I need to say goodbye to my father. I need to move on. That's why I was stealing all those books, to earn enough money to move to San Fran. But then I got caught and my asshole boss tried to blackmail me. I should've just quit and accepted the consequences, but I was stupid and I let him rape me. I was so stupid. I walked right into it. I wanted to tell you, but then you'd kill him, just like you killed Simon. What's wrong with you? How could you cross the line like that? I only asked you to beat him up, maybe knock out a few teeth, but not cut off his fingers! And the one person I want you to destroy, I won't tell you about because I know you'll torture my boss and God knows what kinds of terrible things you'll do to him. It's so fucked up. I'm so fucked up. I don't know what to do anymore. I don't even have any money to leave. I'm stuck in this fucking loft. I'm stuck in this rut. I'm stuck in these fucked-up relationships. I'm stuck with a baby inside of me, and I wished I knew…I knew… who… it belonged to. Deep down, my gut says it's you, but I don't know. Do I want to know? Do you want to know? Maybe it's better that nobody knows. I just wish I could close my eyes and fade away into the darkness… into the nothingness."

Ivan kissed her on the forehead and left the loft. He drove home in a somber silence. Kelly had become the sun in his cold, damp universe. He revolved around her. When she asked him to leave, a tidal wave of depression nearly drowned him. He felt like his chest and abdomen were smashed by sledgehammers. The Ecstasy had worn off, and Ivan stepped off the edge of an emotional cliff after his increased serotonin levels had substantially crashed. It was a nasty side effect of the love drug. When you were flying that high up in the atmosphere, it was inevitable that you'd crash and burn – hard and fast.

Ivan's mood soured when he walked into his apartment and the foul stench from Olga's mother invaded his nostrils. The Old Mule shit herself again. The living room rumbled with Olga's raucous snoring. She had passed out on the couch. An empty Bailey's Irish Cream bottle sat next to an ashtray overflowing with menthol cigarette butts.

Ivan stood over his wife. He could smother her with a pillow and she'd be dead in less than ninety seconds. Tal would know what to do with the body. Then maybe Tal would help him kill Alexi? Ivan wanted him dead – on principle – and while he was at it, he decided to take over Alexi's speed-dealing business.

If cocaine was the drug of choice for the ruling elite of New York, then speed was what fueled the proletariat who kept the city buzzing and humming. In order for the middle class to continue working long hours, especially hacks logging 12-hour shifts, they needed something to give them a little extra pep.

Ivan ransacked the apartment in search of the last drops of liquor. After he slammed the rest of his vodka, he broke into Olga's emergency bottle of Irish Cream, which she stashed in the bathroom underneath the sink. Ivan sat in the dark. He drank and plotted revenge.

Chapter 25

Olga left the apartment before Ivan woke up. He was happy he didn't have to see her ratty eyes, because he might have slit her throat. He called Kelly a couple of times, but she didn't answer. Yuri called Ivan while he was in the shower, but Ivan didn't call him back. Yuri scheduled him to drive a limo later that evening, so he blew off his brother and drove to Williamsburg instead.

Ivan rang the buzzer to Kelly's loft but she didn't answer. He waited for someone to exit and snuck into the building. He banged on her front door and heard her kittens meowing from the other side. It took him fifteen minutes before he finally picked the lock.

He found Kelly on the couch. One of the kittens licked at a pool of caked vomit on the dusty hardwood floor. Her face looked blue and her lips were bright purple. Bits of puke were crusted on her chin. Ivan scooped her up and rushed out of the apartment. He left the door wide open and two of her Siamese kittens scurried down the hallway.

With Kelly's overdosed body in the back of his cab, Ivan sped the entire way to Metropolitan Hospital. He ran two red lights, clipped a gypsy cab, nearly ran down a couple of pissed-off pedestrians, and double-parked in front of the hospital. He rushed into the ER begging for a help. A nurse responded and wheeled Kelly's limp body into a treatment room.

Ivan lied to the admitting nurse and said that Kelly was his daughter. He asked to go inside, but the nurse wouldn't allow it until Kelly's situation stabilized. Ivan agonized in the waiting room for an hour before someone in pink scrubs came outside to talk to him.

"Your daughter is lucky to be alive," deadpanned a nurse as she read off Kelly's chart. "We pumped her stomach. She went to one hell of a party last night. Cocaine. Marijuana. Hashish. Lorazepam. Alprazolam. Klonopin. Oxycodone. Ketamine. Sleeping pills. Prozac."

Ivan looked at Kelly's limp body with tubes sticking out of her arms and nose.

"You're lucky you found her when you did. Another few minutes and she would have choked on her own vomit. She had a rough night for sure. She really needs rest."

The attending physician pulled Ivan aside and lowered his voice. "You better have a talk with your daughter. She better clean up her act. Someone pregnant and in her condition should not be abusing drugs and alcohol. She's lucky she didn't have a miscarriage. She'd better start taking care of herself if you want a healthy grandchild. She needs to visit a therapist and an obstetrician. Understand?"

Ivan fell back into a chair and hyperventilated.

Without any health insurance, the ER released Kelly as soon as she woke up. Ivan drove her back to the loft and put her to bed. He offered to stay behind, but Kelly insisted he return to work. She really meant it that time. After she got some rest, Ivan promised to finally sit down and have a long talk about everything.

Ivan called up Sasha and explained what happened. A hysterical Sasha blitzed him with a series of questions he did not want to answer.

"Daddy, why were you at Kelly's loft?"

"Daddy, why did she do this?"

"Daddy, what were you doing there?"

"Daddy, what is going on with you and Kelly?"

Ivan evaded his daughter's questions. He couldn't reveal the truth even though he knew he should. He suggested they meet later that night and said he'd explain everything. Ivan didn't know what to say. He just wanted to buy some time.

Ivan attempted to clean up Kelly's loft and find her lost kittens that had escaped earlier. Two of the three kittens were AWOL, but Ivan found one. The dried puke on the couch indicated that Kelly's last meal was pasta and carrots. Most of the chunks of undigested food were gobbled up by the kittens. Underneath the couch, Ivan found a McDonald's bag with an empty container of fries and a half-eaten Filet-O-Fish sandwich that upon closer inspection, had been infested by cockroaches. Ivan had not eaten all day and almost took a bite out of the leftovers. It was a good thing he looked at the sandwich before he took chomped down on a Filet-O-Roach.

With Kelly sound asleep, Ivan left the loft. He needed a drink. He needed advice. He needed to see Jimmy the bartender.

Ivan drove to Brooklyn Heights and parked around the corner from the Montague Street Saloon. He sat at the end of the bar, in his usual spot. Jimmy poured Ivan his usual – Stoli on ice with a splash of Sprite. Thoughts of Kelly rattled around his mind. He got flashbacks about the cock sundaes. He liked to pour whipped cream on his dick and Kelly sucked it all off.

Ivan quickly downed his first drink. Jimmy didn't speak a word and poured him another. Ivan felt solely responsible for Kelly's misery and drained the second drink. He didn't notice the Yankees-Red Sox game on the TV. The Yanks were up 7-6 in the bottom of the ninth inning with two outs. Mariano Rivera was in trouble with runners on the corners and Trot Nixon up at the plate. Fervent Yanks fans chanted boisterous beer-fueled anti-Boston taunts, which grew even louder after Rivera struck out Nixon on three straight cut fastballs.

The crowd eventually thinned out after the game ended and Jimmy had a little more time to chat with Ivan.

"You've had four drinks in an hour. You've reached my limit. Either you tell me what's wrong or I'm cutting you off."

"Sasha is marrying a lesbian. My wife is fucking Alexi. My lover is pregnant. She is Sasha's best friend. She tried suicide. Pills. I found her. She survived. Now, I drink."

"Holy Jesus, Mary, and Joseph. I've known you for 12, no 13 years, right Ivan? Since I've known you, you've always gotten into fucked-up situations. It was a matter of time before everything caught up to you. Right now, you have to take control of your life. Talk to your brother. You need his help. I know you two don't get along, but you need someone in your family who will actually help you. If you want my advice? You need to divorce your wife. Send the cow back home to Russia. You need to take that girlfriend of yours to the doctor and get her fixed. Then you have to stop seeing her, especially if she's your daughter's friend. And your daughter? All I can say is be happy that she found someone, lesbian or not. If she wants to get married, so be it. Hey, marrying a woman is a lot better than some punk-ass crackhead with green hair, right? Be happy for her. Be happy yourself. If all of these women cause you so much heartache, then you need to let them all go. Release your grip on them and you release all your stress."

Ivan nodded. Jimmy always knew the right thing to say. Forty years behind a bar gave a man like that clarity on life.

"Release," mumbled Ivan.

"Release them all," said Jimmy as he pouted Ivan another stiff drink.

Chapter 26

Early evening. Ivan stumbled down Montague Street on one of those hot and testy, bustling, summer Sunday nights in New York. He passed the bodegas and the hipsters in the cigar shops. At a crowded outdoor café, he almost knocked over a yuppie couple with a stroller.

Ivan barreled into the front door of the Montague Car Service Company. He rushed by the receptionist and Alexi the dispatcher. Ivan whirled around and glared at Alexi. Ivan fell into a trance and his mind drifted off into a fantasy world as he stood motionless with a blank stare, while images of destruction festered around his brain. He wanted to shoot Alexi in the kneecaps, then tie him up with duct tape. He wanted to make thousands of tiny paper cuts and pour lemon juice on them. He wanted to make Alexi scream. He wanted to make Olga watch him slice off pieces of Alexi's flesh and force her to eat it on a hotdog bun. Ivan wanted to mutilate Alexi with ice picks and screwdrivers. He wanted to dismantle Alexi's skull with a Swiss Army knife. He wanted to cut off his toes and feed them to the ducks in Central Park. He wanted to throw Alexi off the Brooklyn Bridge. He wanted to hammer a rusted four-inch railroad spike through Alexi's scrotum. He wanted to scoop out Alexi's eyeballs with melon-ball slicers. Ivan acquired various torture techniques while working for Pytor and his thugs. He wanted to use all of them.

Ivan snapped out of his daze and rushed toward Yuri's office.

"Don't go in there!" screamed the receptionist.

Ivan wiggled the doorknob. Locked. He took two steps back, then kicked the door in, like in a police raid. The door flew open and Ivan puked in the hallway. Yuri sat behind his desk with his pants around his ankles, a young Korean girl from the nail salon next door servicing him.

Pytor used the salon as one of many fronts where he washed cash he earned from running massage parlors and escort services. Pytor also owned a piece of a flourishing Russian mail-order bride website, which itself was a front for a human trafficking ring. Aside from the salon and the limo company, Yuri also managed two of Pytor's gambling ventures – an illegal casino in Coney Island and an underground poker club in Sunset Park. Ivan was a sucker for no-limit Texas Hold 'em and spent most of his free time losing his shirt against crazy Asian gamblers. Yuri banned Ivan from one of the poker clubs earlier that summer when Ivan went berserk and beat the shit out of a dealer when he lost a $900 hand.

"Ivan you fucking pig!"

Yuri zipped up his pants and motioned for the Korean girl to leave through the back door. Ivan hunched over and dry heaved. Yuri walked over and kicked him in the stomach. Ivan puked up a greenish glob of bile. Yuri bitch-slapped Ivan. A glob of yellow saliva stuck to the tip of his brother's nose.

"Are you drunk? You showed up to drive drunk? You have no respect!"

Yuri stepped back and prepared to fight his brother. Ivan just rolled over on the floor with an emotionally vacant stare.

"You're fucking useless," Yuri barked in Russian. "You were always the big fuck up, Ivan, do you know that? Ever since you were a little boy. You always got in trouble. Not because you were bad, but because you were stupid. Mother was right. You're a dumbass. I felt sorry for you, that's why I begged Pytor to give you a job when you came to America. And he took care of you. I took care of you. But how do you pay us back? By acting like a drunk fool. Your best talent in life seems to be fucking up things that are already fucked up. You've embarrassed me more times than I can count."

Yuri fired Ivan on the spot.

Ivan picked himself up, walked into Yuri's office and locked the door. Ivan dropped his pants and shit on Yuri's desk. He also urinated on his chair before Yuri could get inside. Ivan ran out the back door. When he got to his cab, he called the only person who could help him. Tal.

Less than an hour later, Tal met Ivan at Veselka, an Eastern European diner in the East Village. The two had an intense two-hour talk, more like a confession of sins. Ivan told Tal everything. Everything. Including the story about Kelly's suicide attempt and his thoughts on how to torture Alexi. Tal didn't have much advice on marriage because he never married.

"Relationships are tough no matter how you look at them," Tal told Ivan. "But with Kelly, if you really love her, you have to follow your heart, no matter what your daughter says or society thinks."

Ivan asked Tal to watch his back. He was worried that Pytor would put a hit out on him.

"I wouldn't worry about Yuri and Pytor. They're a bunch of wanna-be gangsters on the verge of getting pinched by the Feds. I was eventually going to tell you that the heat was closing in, but now is a perfect chance to break away from them. Otherwise, you're going to end up in jail, or worse, thrown into the secret prison in Cuba."

Tal told Ivan he'd gladly wipe out Alexi using a rogue group of female assassins from Mossad.

"One of my girls will accidentally meet Alexi at a bar," assured Tal. "They are so beautiful and so seductive. He'll be so enamored with her beauty he won't suspect a thing. She'll lure him out to Red Hook and we'll do the rest. For $5,000, I can have his penis delivered to you in a mason jar."

Ivan nodded his head. Even if he had to go into debt to Tal, it was well worth the price for revenge. The package deal also included the "mop up" guys – Albanian fishermen from Breezy Point, who disposed of dead bodies by cutting up limbs into little pieces of bait.

Chapter 27

When Ivan stopped by the loft, Kelly was watching *Seinfeld*, the episode where Kramer and his attorney, the honorable Jackie Childs, unsuccessfully sued a Big Tobacco company for turning Kramer's face into a hideous monster.

Kelly turned off the TV and finally had the talk with Ivan that she had been putting off for months. She told him everything she had written in the letter during a grueling four-hour tear-ridden monologue.

"I couldn't afford an abortion, so I figured if I did enough drugs, I'd have a miscarriage. Either way, it'd be sentencing someone to murder again. First it was Simon, and now with whatever is crawling around inside me."

"I want to marry you. I want to have this child. I want to be a father."

"Ivan, please to come to your senses!" sobbed Kelly.

Ivan thought he was doing the right thing by divorcing Olga and marrying Kelly to make an honest woman out of her. But she didn't want any part of motherhood or marriage. She made her decision to have an abortion and told Ivan it would be best if they stopped seeing each other.

"You have to leave Ivan," she practically begged. "If you love me, you'll leave."

She explained that she needed to be alone for a while, a long time, and needed time to grieve the fact that she watched her father's murder live on CNN.

A stunned and perplexed Ivan did not know what to say. He arrived at the loft thinking he was about to start a new life with Kelly with a shot at being a competent parent. Instead, he got dumped and told that the love of his life, the one person who made him feel the most warmth he'd ever felt, didn't ever want to see him again.

Ivan did not fight Kelly. He accepted defeat and said a tearful goodbye before he shuffled off to his cab. He replayed their conversation in his head. He tried to figure out what had just happened. During their talk, Kelly finally revealed the suppressed story about the evil Ken Murphy, her scumbag boss from Barnes and Noble, who sexually assaulted her after he busted up their theft ring. Ivan's fists clenched, his blood pressure rose, and his mind became instantly fixated on avenging his lover's rape.

* * *

Sasha agreed to meet Ivan in a park at the end of 77th Street, overlooking the FDR Drive and the East River. It was the first time he'd seen his daughter since 9/11. She looked beautiful. "A miracle," he thought, how the daughter of a short and ugly man and a beast of a woman like Olga, herself the offspring of the "Old Mule," managed to be one of the most beautiful people he had ever seen.

Sasha's medium-length brown hair looked perfect in the city twilight. She could have been a shampoo model from one of those commercials. She wore a white tank top and a green and blue pastel miniskirt. Ivan noticed a small tattoo on her left ankle – a red heart with an arrow through the center.

"Sasha is a heartbreaker, for sure," he thought.

Ivan ruined lives. He murdered an unknown number of people from many different countries, on many continents, and in many different ways. But none of those blemishes on his soul could block out the radiant aura of his daughter. A wave of pride washed over Ivan. As much pain and suffering he thrust into the world, he finally saw something positive come out of it. Sasha.

Ivan had his moment with Sasha where he told her everything. It took almost five hours, but he told her about her Sweet Sixteen party and his first incident with Kelly. He told her about catching Olga fucking Alexi. He told her about his first wife's blind sister Petra. He told her about killing the British guy who managed Kelly's boyfriend's band. He told her that after Kelly dumped him, he considered jumping off the Brooklyn Bridge.

Sasha sat in restrained silence most of the time Ivan rambled on with his confessions. Eventually, it was Sasha's turn to talk, and Ivan listened. She told Ivan about everything she had kept secret from him, like the relationship with Kelly, the hand jobs to neighborhood boys for slices of pizza, and allowing a nun at St. Cecilia's High School finger her for $5 a session. She told Ivan about her own misadventures in the city's bizarre S&M world, along with the occasional tricks she turned to support her former boyfriend's band. She also told Ivan the story about how she knew for a fact that her girlfriend Amanda was her soulmate.

Ivan sat and listened to his daughter reveal herself to him. He realized that if he had been a better father, more nurturing and supportive, that maybe Sasha would not have experienced so much pain and hardship in her life. Decades of backed-up guilt, sorrow, and shame made his knees weak. It almost felt like he was having a heart attack when he acknowledged the fact that he had been a major failure as a father. He probably fucked up his first kid, Nikolai, who never spoke to him, and he knew how screwed up Sasha turned out.

"I'm sorry," Ivan said. After a while, that's all he could say, but that time, he truly meant it after becoming encompassed in sorrow.

Ivan and Sahsa held hands as the sun rose above the city and the glistening hues of yellow and orange sunlight bounced off the water, which made the East River look like it was overflowing with gems and little stars. For the first time in a very long time, the tumultuous waters that raged between them had dwindled to a mellow, soothing trickle.

Chapter 28

Ivan parked his cab a few blocks from his apartment in Park Slope. He looked at the clock. 6:54 a.m. He spent the entire evening and early morning with his daughter. They had an actual conversation for the first time in both their lives, and they definitely found a common ground – they both hated Olga, and both loved Kelly.

Sasha understood something about Kelly that Ivan didn't – that she needed to complete the grieving process with her father. As much as Sasha could have created a life with Kelly, she felt as though Kelly needed to live a life of her own. In a way, Sasha was doing the best thing for Kelly. At least, that's how Sasha explained it to Ivan, and why she insisted that Ivan leave Kelly alone, at least for a while until she cleared her head.

Ivan walked up the stairs to his apartment and noticed the unlocked front door. He didn't think anything of it because sometimes Olga left the door unlocked if she ran down to the corner bodega to buy cigarettes, although perhaps he should have because she was usually at work by 6 a.m. Besides, the Old Mule never left the apartment. If anyone was brave enough to enter that foul-smelling place and try to steal something while the Old Mule watched *Little House on the Prairie* in the living room, then they were more than welcome to take what they pleased.

Ivan took a couple of steps into his apartment when he felt a sharp pain in the back of his head and neck. He was hit hard by an aluminum Little League baseball bat. His knees caved in and he fell to the floor. He blacked out, but when he eventually came to a few moments later, his pockets were being emptied by someone he could not recognize. Blood gushed from a gash over his right eye, which blurred his vision and covered his face.

Pedro (the flamboyant, transvestite hotdog vendor from Waverly Place) took all the money out of Ivan's wallet, $86, and dragged his bulky body into the bedroom by pulling his foot. Pedro had already silenced Ivan's mother-in-law. He broke into the apartment when the Old Mule was in the bathroom changing her adult diaper. It only took one swing of the bat to turn her brains into mush. She died just like Elvis – face down, ass up in the bathroom.

When Ivan regained consciousness, Pedro jammed him in the ribs with the bat. He heard something crack.

"We wanted to get married," Pedro screamed. "You killed my lover! My hot panda bear of a lover."

A devastated Pedro vowed revenge for the death of Simon, the Toothless Tool from Liverpool. He instantly suspected that the neo-hippie beatniks from Jack Tripper Stole My Dog had something to do with Simon's disappearance, so Pedro followed them up to New Hampshire. He knew the exact motel where Simon had booked them to stay during the Mountain Jam music festival. He waited until their after-party died down before he struck. While the band members were all passed out, he snuck into Kelly's boyfriend's room, tied him up, and tortured the hairy arm-pitted groupie that occupied his bed. She screamed and pleaded for Pedro to stop beating her with a Gideon's Bible. He spit in her face and bashed her skull. Most of the New Testament became soaked with her splattered blood and brain matter.

Pedro poured gasoline over Kelly's boyfriend and threatened to light his dreadlocks on fire unless he gave up the name of Simon's killer. He quickly blurted out Ivan's name. Pedro did not show him any mercy. He tossed a match at the dreadlocks and Kelly's boyfriend burned to death while bound to a chair.

Pedro fled the motel after killing five of the original members of Jack Tripper Stole My Dog, their new tour manager, the drummer's twin brother, and four dosed-out groupies. Pedro left the bloody bible behind to confuse authorities, who instantly suspected that the murders were religiously motivated. By the time the New Hampshire State Police discovered all of the bodies from the burning rubble and notified the local press about the bloody bible, Pedro had already broken into Ivan's apartment in Brooklyn and teed off on the Old Mule's noggin.

Pedro sat on the edge of the bed, ready to cut Ivan's eyes out with a scalpel.

"You don't know what it's like to want to be with someone, but you can't!"

Actually, thought Ivan, he knew exactly what Pedro meant.

"Now, you will pay for your sins!" screeched Pedro, ready to plunge a sharp instrument into Ivan's ocular cavity.

Pedro froze. He heard a noise in the living room and jumped up. Someone walked into the apartment. Before Pedro could confront the intruder in the living room, he was shot twice in the chest. Pedro fell dead, slumped over Ivan's favorite chair, the one where he loved to watch TV.

* * *

Ivan awoke in the hospital two days later. He was greeted by a splitting headache and a familiar face – Tal.

Ivan's head was bandaged after fracturing his skull. His jaw was also wired shut. Ivan couldn't talk and was in severe, vision-blurring pain. A large nurse stormed into the room to increase Ivan's morphine drip.

"I'm sure you're wondering what the fuck happened."

Ivan nodded slightly. He was in too much pain to move his head.

"Well, after our long talk," explained Tal. "I knew you weren't in a good head space. I followed you to make sure you didn't do anything stupid like kill yourself. Once you got home, I figured you were OK. I was ready to leave, but that's when I heard the screaming and rushed upstairs. The guy who jumped you was that hotdog freak, you know, the faggot who went out with the British band manager? Well, you fucked up by disposing the corpse in the Central Park Reservoir. A jogger saw the body and called the cops. Pedro discovered the murder a lot sooner than he was supposed to. I mean, you were trying to make it look like the British guy disappeared, but you got too carried away. Those things happened, but you underestimated the strength of the faggot. You should have taken him out too. That's what I would have done. Ah, that's hindsight. Anyway, the little hotdog tranny tracked down the band somewhere in New England. He tortured them and those pansies ratted you out as Simon's killer. Pedro didn't let the band off easily. He torched them all. He beat one girl's brains in with a Bible. The local newspapers ran the story and every media outlet, even CNN, picked it up. They've become fascinated with the Pedro killings. It's the next sensationalized American crime story."

Tal showed Ivan a copy of the New York Daily News. The cover had a picture of Pedro and the headline: *Brooklyn Cabbie Survives Attack from Tranny Bible Killer.*

"The police want to talk to you, but I already took care of the finer points. Just so you know, I shot Pedro. Dropped him like a cold fish. Pow. Pow. Two shots. He went down. I put the gun in your hands, so it looked like self-defense. All you have to do is just tell the cops, on the record, that you don't remember anything. NYPD wants to pin Simon's murder on Pedro, so you're off the hook on that one. Oh, and you got lucky. Pedro whacked your mother-in-law too. Now you don't have to worry about the Old Donkey."

"Ooooool," Ivan tried to speak Olga's name.

"Olga?" explained Tal. "She's cooperating and willingly returning to the Ukraine. I showed her the mason jar with Alexi's dick in it, and she started packing right away."

Chapter 29

It took three months before Ivan could drive his cab part-time. He wanted to resume his old schedule, but slogging 12-hour shifts while hopped up on painkillers wasn't exactly the responsible thing for Ivan to do. Alas, he missed his routine and tried to regain a life of normalcy after his unexpected brush with fame. Ivan loved New York City. There was no other place he'd rather be. He got a second chance at life when he fled Russia and came to America. After he screwed that up, he got a rare third chance at life. He didn't want that to slip through his fingers.

Ivan had become a micro-celebrity for his run-in with the Bible Beater Serial Killer. Ivan appeared on the talk show circuit – *Larry King Live*, *The O'Reilly Factor*, *The View*, Court TV, Fox News, BBC News, and even a slot on Dr. Phil's show. Ivan's agent fetched him a book deal with Simon & Schuster, who wanted to publish his life story. They even hired a ghost writer, an out-of-work creative writing student from NYU, to interview Ivan and write a first draft.

Ivan took his book advance and instead of paying for his mounting medical bills, he gave most of the money to Kelly. He surprised her at work one day. He didn't say anything and just handed her the envelope. He hugged her goodbye before she could open it up. Inside was a blank postcard from San Francisco and $10,000 in cash.

Sasha and Amanda postponed their big day until Ivan's health improved and he could attend the wedding. He took a liking to Amanda, who helped nurse him back to health by bringing over Ben & Jerry's chocolate milkshakes and bottles of Stoli.

Ivan looked at the clock. 4:20 p.m. In Tribeca, he loaded a nerdy-looking guy, who requested Columbia University. Ivan immediately recognized him. He was the Bill Gates lookalike who that told him Bea Arthur was a CIA agent.

"You can't go anywhere anymore without being watched. Even your cabs have cameras now. When I take the subway, all my movements are recorded. Whenever I walk into a store, my image is captured on surveillance cameras. When I take out cash at an ATM, or even walk past one, they can find me. Penn Station. Grand Central Station. No matter where I go, there *They* are."

Ivan chuckled, then sipped his flask.

"I read a book that some Australian crackpot wrote suggesting Stephen King was the real gunman in John Lennon's murder and that Mark David Chapman was just a patsy. Either Nixon or Reagan had Lennon whacked. They both hated him. Nixon had wanted to deport Lennon in the 1970s when he brashly criticized Nixon's foreign policy in Southeast Asia. Lennon was also in hot water with Reagan, or shall I say the real puppet master, George Hebert Walker Bush. We all know that Bush held three terms as President from 1980 to 1992, and again with his idiot son in power. Reagan was just a puppet, especially after *They* tried to have him killed. You know that George Bush used to be the head of the CIA?"

Ivan shook his head.

"The Bush Junta are bad motherfuckers who were involved in all kinds of deep shit back in the 1970s, including running heroin out of Asia and funding covert operations and regime changes all over the world. Uganda, Zaire, Peru, Argentina, Laos, the Ivory Coast."

"Clinton good?" asked Ivan.

"He's a bad motherfucker too. The entire Monica Lewinsky thing was just a cover-up for some really shady business that had been going on, like Whitewater and all those so-called friends of Clinton that were mysteriously found dead like Ron Brown and three of Clinton's bodyguards, and everyone else close to Clinton that died over the last twenty years. William Jefferson Clinton. Bubba Clinton. Now, there's something to talk about. A lot of people think Bubba was helping run the largest cocaine smuggling ring in 1980s America. They made movies and wrote books about Pablo Escobar and George Jung, but they should have wrote one about Bubba. His code name was *Snowflake*. He allowed the CIA to fly in and out of small airports all over Arkansas when he was Governor Bubba. They flew roundtrips to and from South America doing coke runs. He then distributed the blow to all corners of America. Shit, Bubba was one of the biggest importers of cocaine in the history of the War on Drugs."

"Is *They* and the CIA the same?"

"Good question," said Bill Gates. "*They* are businessmen and bankers who are independent of the CIA, but the CIA is essentially their intelligence wing. Sometimes they hire out private special forces who do all of the dirty work. Assassination squads. Look what happened in the 1960s. First, JFK got whacked. Then his brother, Bobby. Then Martin Luther King. Then Malcolm X. Then the leaders of the Black Panthers. Then *They* got to the biggest union figure in America, Jimmy Hoffa. Hoffa went missing and was never found. There's an urban myth that he's buried underneath the endzone at Giants stadium. I don't believe it. *They* probably shot him, then fed his corpse to the dogs. The guys pulling the strings, they feared the people when they were led by dangerous political figures. But once you removed the self-righteous politicians, you removed any chance of real change. These days, every politician plays ball. They're all on the take, otherwise they know that their melons will be used for target practice like the Kennedys. But now, *They* have to fight the biggest fight they have ever faced. Fundamentalist Islam. Those radicals are violent fuckers. Oh my. The CIA knew it back in the 1960s when Islam first reached America and the intelligence community used their best and swiftest methods to combat the rise in fundamentalist religious fervor and keep Allah out of the ghettos. Look what was happening in the 1960s: protests, race riots, and people standing up and saying 'fuck you' to the establishment. But then Islam comes along, which freaked the fuck out of the Man. It was like throwing plutonium onto a grease fire. They didn't want messages from Allah reaching poor blacks in the ghetto and persuading them to join the Islam Revolution. The radical aspects of Islam taught hatred towards Jews and Christians with the white man as the devil figure in their eyes. They wanted to squash any rebellion as fast as they could, so how do you stop millions of people from looting and rioting and adhering to the only rule they knew – anarchy? It was simple actually. Chemical. That's it. Everybody must get stoned. Dylan said it best, man. Everyone must get stoned. They are doing it today with the internet and did it yesterday with TV and Hollywood. But in the 1960s, the CIA knew they needed to get all those fringe people calmed down. So they got them high. They had a huge supply of smack in Asia and they introduced their product into a new market – the ghettos. They flooded the United States with heroin, especially the volatile urban areas of Los Angeles, Detroit, Chicago, St. Louis, New York City, Atlanta, Birmingham, and Memphis. The CIA used Air America pilots to fly guns and weapons into Cambodia and Laos, then take opium back to the States. When the kids in the ghetto took a few hits of China White, they were hooked, and all of a sudden the raging fire of fervent religious fundamentalism and social change slowly calmed to a smoldering fizzle of apathy and laziness. People got high instead of protesting. It was more important to get your fix than stand up to the Man. The ghettos were filled with functioning addicts, those who need drugs to survive, yet assimilated into society holding jobs and families in order to get the necessary means to keep their habit going. Today, *They* created a War on Terror to exterminate religious fundamentalism, the hugest threat to our capitalist way of living that we have ever seen. It's a bigger threat than Communism ever was. If we don't figure out how to contain it, we are doomed. New York will look like Jerusalem. Car bombs and bus bombs. Martial law. Agents from Homeland Security knocking down doors looking for these homegrown terrorists. Believe me, that's what will happen in ten years unless we start getting the extremists hooked on a heroin again, or we must go in and wipe them all out. Either way, I'm moving to Iceland."

Epilogue

Ivan's cab waited in front of a pool hall in Koreatown. A woman with long silky blonde hair rushed out and slid into the backseat. She wore tight clothing, exposing her athletic figure. Ivan handed her an envelope and a mason jar. Ivan drove to Union Square and she opened up the envelope. She studied two photographs of her target.

Ivan unloaded Svetlana, who didn't pay for the fare. She wandered through the farmer's market on the north end of Union Square and smoked two cigarettes. She made a call on a pay phone, then walked into Barnes and Noble.

Store manager Ken Murphy was training a new employee, a grad student at NYU, who politely deflected any of his blatant advances. She'd eventually share her awkward story with other female employees, all of whom were sexually harassed by Murphy at one time or another. Because that store had an employee turnover rate in excess of 80%, no one was there long enough to actually file a legitimate claim against him.

Svetlana watched Murphy. She carefully followed him around the store maintaining a safe distance, as he wandered up and down aisles and through the different sections leering at employees and customers. She left the bookstore and walked across the square to the Heartland Brewery. She ordered two shots of whiskey and downed them. She found a bench in the park and waited until Barnes and Noble closed.

Svetlana waited for Murphy to exit the building. She pulled out a tourist's map of New York City and purposely bumped into him.

"Pardon me," Svetlana cooed in a fake French accent, "I am lost. Can you tell me where zee Greenwich Village is?"

Murphy locked his eyes onto Svetlana's large chest. Her curves became magnets for Murphy's depraved glances. She hooked him instantly. After a few moments of flirting, Svetlana convinced Murphy to buy her a drink at a dive bar around the corner. They sat in the back and Murphy felt like the biggest swinging dick north of Wall Street, because he picked up a hot French tourist. Murphy was positive he was going to get laid because of the way she stroked his arm when he told her about different books he claimed to have read, but had never even picked up once. He hadn't had sex since he date raped a Venezuelan nanny a few months earlier. His mother set him up when she stopped by for dinner at her house. He offered her a cocktail in his basement apartment, and she foolishly followed him into his dungeon. He slipped her some GHB and she passed out. It had been a months since he had a mouthful of high-octane South American pussy and he was horny as hell.

One drink turned into four, until Svetlana abruptly said she had to leave. Murphy grew agitated. He hated losing power struggles to women. He demanded to know where she was going. She calmly explained that she had to meet a friend at a gallery opening in Brooklyn. Svetlana suggested he should join her.

They hailed a taxi and Svetlana gave the driver an address in Red Hook. The cab sped south down Broadway and they groped each other in the backseat. As the cab headed over the Brooklyn Bridge, Svetlana unzipped Murphy's pants and began jerking him off. She stopped after a few seconds and told him to save it.

"You French bitches are a cock tease," grumbled Murphy.

They kissed during the remainder of the ride (which entailed Murphy slobbering all over Svetlana) until the cab let them off in a remote section of Red Hook by a series of abandoned warehouses. Svetlana made Murphy pay the $28 cab ride.

"What the fuck is this place?" Murphy asked.

"My cousin Marie lives in one of zees lofts. I have to stop by her place, before we can go to zee party."

Svetlana and Murphy rode the freight elevator to the third floor. She led him into an alcove and then pulled down his pants.

"I want to watch you touch yourself," she ordered.

Murphy quickly compiled.

"Faster!" she screamed. Murphy did not notice that she dropped her French accent.

Murphy jerked himself off with an increased velocity. He rubbed furiously.

"I want you to come for me. Now!"

A stream of sweat ran down Murphy's face as he reached a climax. He ejaculated on the ground. Svetlana smiled, then ordered him to lick it up.

"Fuck this," he moaned.

"Do it now," screamed Svetlana, as she revealed her right breast. "Otherwise, I will not show you the other one."

Murphy bent over and began lapping up his own semen.

"You've been a good boy. I want to blindfold you while I blow you," she said.

Svetlana removed his t-shirt and created a makeshift blindfold that she wrapped around his head. His sticky uncircumcised penis hardened.

"Suck it now," he demanded.

Svetlana yanked on his shaft with her left hand. She reached into her bag with the right hand and removed a concealed knife. She squeezed his minuscule penis in her hand and whispered into his ear.

"I can't hear you," Murphy said.

"This is for Kelly," she said, before she plunged the blade into his testicles.

Author's Note and Acknowledgments

In November of 2002, at the insistence of my friend Jessica Lapidus, I signed up for National Novel Writing Month (NaNoWriMo), a writing project in which the participants have a single month to complete a 50,000-word novel. I wrote the first draft of *Jack Tripper Stole My Dog* in ten days. Although NaNoWriMo was a success, I did not pick up the manuscript for nearly four years.

In the autumn of 2006, I revisited *Jack Tripper Stole My Dog* and wrote a second draft. I waited another four years or so before I attempted a third and final draft.

In the current version of *Jack Tripper Stole My Dog*, I felt obligated to preserve the original story that I attempted to tell in November 2002. At the time, I lived in New York City and worked down the street from Ground Zero. The NaNoWriMo novel became an outlet for many bottled-up emotions about my own life while formulating my world view in post-9/11 America. That's why I felt it was essential that the novel took place in 2002 (instead of updating it to the present). It was a unique and weird time in history – a few weeks before the first anniversary of 9/11 and six months before the Iraq War started.

And now it's time to say thanks…

Without a doubt, the biggest thanks goes out to my amazing girlfriend K.B. a.k.a. "Nicky" for putting up with my nonsense during the re-write, editing, and publishing phase. She also deserves credit for taking the time out of her schedule to edit *Jack Tripper Stole My Dog*.

Thanks to Jessica Lapidus for encouraging me to take a leap of faith with NaNoWriMo. And of course, many thanks to NaNoWriMo for instilling discipline in a lost writer.

I never would have gotten to where I am today without the support, cash, and love of my brother, Derek McGuire. In Johnny Drama's voice: "Thanks, baby bro!"

Thanks to the Emory crew: Dave Simanoff, David Sheer, Jerry Engel, Armando Huerta, Jonathan Schanzer, and Brad Singer.

Thanks to AlCantHang for being AlCantHang.

Special thanks to my proofreaders: Nicky, Derek, Jessica, Neil Fontenot, and Jeremiah Schupbach.

Thanks to Kat Goodale for the amazing cover art and thanks to Kym Bracken for the author's photo.

Thanks to Dr. Ken Friedman for helping me become a better writer.

Lastly, I want to extend a huge, all-encompassing thank you to all of my friends and family for their unwavering support over the years. I can definitely be an asshole, especially when I'm writing, so thanks for being patient and understanding.

Paul McGuire

(Los Angeles, CA, May 2011)

About the Author

Paul 'Dr. Pauly' McGuire is a writer originally from New York City and currently resides in Los Angeles, CA. McGuire is the author of *Lost Vegas: The Redneck Riviera, Existentialist Conversations with Strippers, and the World Series of Poker.*

If you would like to read more from Paul McGuire, visit...

Lost Vegas – lostvegasbook.com

Tao of Pauly – taopauly.com

Tao of Poker – taopoker.com

Tao of Fear – taofear.com

Coventry Music – phish-coventry.com

Truckin' – mcgtruckin.blogspot.com

Tao of Bacon – taobacon.com

For future news about *Jack Tripper Stole My Dog*, follow @JackTripperBook on Twitter. You can always visit the website www.jackripperstolemydog.com for updates and other information.